Bulletproof GODS

Money Over Everything

2

A NOVEL BY

TYSHA JORDYN, SHAMEKA JONES

& VIRGO

CHAPTER 1

Zeus

Never let another muthafucka see you sweat.

My father's words rang in my ears as the barrel of the gun pressed harder into my back, threatening to become one with my spine. I could not believe that we'd walked into the middle of a setup. I was still at a loss as to how we were caught slipping.

"*Siéntate!*" my captor said, pressing the gun further into back.

I grimaced as he burrowed the gun deeper into my back in an attempt to steer me to the seat located across from Titan. I could see the blank expression on his face, but I could also hear his fingers drumming against the armrest.

"*What the fuck?*" Titan tapped out in Morse code.

"*Chill. We will figure something out,*" I tapped back.

Frank DiBiasi knew what the fuck he was doing when he'd trained us. We could have a whole conversation without opening our mouths. Our father taught us Morse code as a means to communicate when cell phones could not be used.

The gunmen paced silently as if they were waiting for a cue to move forward with their plan. I wondered why they had not killed us as they already had the upper hand. Santiago was not one to get his hands dirty, but I knew he would make an exception to the rule when dealing with us. Our demise would have to come directly from his hands, or he would not get the respect he so desperately craved.

I took a few deep breaths and gathered my thoughts. This hiccup was a definite inconvenience. I had a wife that was about to give birth to my first son that I needed to get to. I was more annoyed than shook at the fact that Santiago thought that he could get one over on me by sending in his flunkies. That's where he and I differed. If I had shit that needed to be handled, I had no problem with stepping into battle with my troops and fucking shit up.

"*You strapped?*" Titan tapped, and I nodded curtly in response. "*How do you want to handle this?*"

I cut my eyes around to study my surroundings. Our three would-be captors still had their guns trained on us, and Ares had a gun to his head, so I could not risk drawing my own heat. Judging by the soft whimpers that were coming from the galley area, I assumed the fourth gunman had our flight attendant hemmed up. I knew she was probably scared shitless, so I made a note to compensate her for her pain and suffering—if we made it out of this alive. For once, I did not have a plan. I was so focused on getting to my wife that I did not bother to think about Santiago retaliating against us.

"So, this is it, esé? We just gon' sit here with guns on us?" I asked the one with the gun on me.

"Quiet!" he shouted with his thick accent. "You don't speak. We're waiting on our orders."

I smirked. It was just as I thought. Santiago intended to finish us off on his own. At least he was not the coward I thought him to be. Now, all that was left to do was figure out how to get the upper hand.

"I see," I said quietly as I smirked to Titan, and he smirked back. I shot a look over to Ares, and he looked like he was ready to start smoking from his ears at any moment.

I knew that the situation could go from bad to worse at any moment, so I had to think fast. My burner was pressing against my stomach. I was surprised that I still had it in my possession because it was a rookie mistake of my would-be captors not to check us for weapons. I did not want to reach for it suddenly with Ares being in the predicament that he was in. I was a quick shot, but I knew I would not be able to take these three niggas out in a split second. That shit only happened in movies, or in those hood books that Zo read all the time.

I needed a distraction. We needed something that would take the focus off us for a few seconds so that we could get to our heat and turn the tables. But what? We couldn't reach for our phones to call for back-up. The only other radio was in the cockpit with Santino's dead ass.

Fuck! I thought to myself as I rubbed my hands together and said a silent prayer to God. I was going straight to a confessional if I got out of this alive. I was going to make sure that Titan and Ares went too.

I looked around the plane's cabin once more, trying to devise a plan. Nothing came to mind, and this was a first. I was about to give up formulating a plan and try shooting our way through the bullshit when

I saw a black van pull up on the tarmac. I figured it had to be Santiago coming to put us to sleep. Little did he know, I was not going to let us go out like that.

"*He's here,*" I tapped to Titan.

"*Let's get this shit over with,*" he tapped back. He rolled his eyes at the thought of having to get physical.

My brother did not mind putting in work, but he was more of a tech guy. He liked working behind the scenes. He left the heavy lifting to Ares and me. He always said that his degree from MIT was better served being the eyes and ears of the operation. I always took it as talk that he was too pretty to throw hands. I always gave him a hard time about it.

I focused my attention on Ares, and he was staring straight ahead. I could see the veins throbbing in his temples. My brother was thirty-eight hot. I knew once I gave him the go-ahead to let loose, these esés would feel his wrath and then some. I did not want to bring attention to ourselves, but I had to get his attention.

PSSST!

I made a hissing sound between my teeth to get Ares' attention. He looked at me with annoyance on his face as I dropped my gaze to my hand. His eyes followed, and I made a small gun symbol with my fingers. Ares nodded in understanding and patted the bag in the seat next to him before patting his waist. I chuckled a little bit at the fact that my little brother walked around with a full gun rack on him. I pointed my index finger at myself to let him know to make his move on my signal, and he nodded in understanding.

I knew I had to act fast. Santiago would be stepping on the plane at any moment, and I wanted to put this situation to rest once and for all. There was no sense in prolonging the inevitable. Only one side could survive and really run Miami, and if it were up to me, the DiBiasi family would be that side for many years to come.

Everything had to be timed perfectly. I did not have a doubt in my mind that Ares would be able to take down his captor if offered the slightest window of opportunity. I had to get him that window. Once the gun was off his head, Ares would be able to knock the gun from his hand and grab his own, or... at least, that was the plan. There was a high possibility that shit could go left and someone could get hurt, but we had to try something. My son was coming into the world.

I glanced out of the window, and whoever was in the black van still had not gotten out of it. I did not know what they were waiting on, but we had to make our move before they decided to board our jet. I started the mental countdown in my head. My brothers' eyes were planted on me, waiting for my go-ahead. I held up three fingers and let them know that we would make our move on the count of three before focusing my attention back on the black van. There was still no movement, so I dropped one finger, leaving two up. Our captors had not noticed my small movements. I glanced at Titan and saw the grim expression that laced his face. Anticipation covered Ares' face. He was ready for war.

I looked out the window once more and finally saw the door open. My heartbeat sped up as I watched a pair of black Louboutin dress shoes step out of the car. I still could not see a face, but that did

5

not matter because I knew whoever was getting out of the van meant to end our lives. I dropped another finger and was down to one. Once I closed my fist, we would act. I kept my eyes glued to the tarmac. I wanted whoever it was to walk into chaos. Just as I was about to drop my last finger, an evil smile spread across my lips.

My nigga!

Looking dapper as ever, Bones and I immediately made eye contact, and he gave me a head nod before slipping back into the van. The passenger window rolled down and Knowledge, Titan's right-hand, gave me the thumbs up. I knew they had something up their sleeves. Since I knew that our captors were waiting on word from their boss to act, I knew that we had time because these niggas couldn't make a decision for themselves if their lives depended on it. I opened my entire hand up to stop the countdown. Both Ares and Titan raised their brows at me in disbelief. I discreetly nodded my head out of my window. Ares was across the aisle and could not see, but Titan could.

"*Who's out there?*" he tapped.

"*Knowledge and Bones,*" I tapped back.

A wicked smile spread across his lips.

CHAPTER 2

Titan

*W*ith the exception of some nigga laying hands on the any of the women in our family, I don't think the stakes could have been any higher than they were at the moment—which is why I was glad we had dudes like Bones and Knowledge on our team. They had a mindset that I'd tried to explain to every young knucklehead we brought onboard—a mentality that Pops had started drilling into our heads from an early age: *don't anticipate your enemy's next move, BE the next move.* In that moment, I was just glad that we had some thorough dudes on our team, and that their asses pulled up on us just in the nick of time.

I didn't know what Zeus was on when he paused his countdown, especially knowing that Ares was not the type of nigga you could just say "never mind" to. Giving Ares even the slightest hint that it was go time and then expecting him to pump the brakes was like Obama pressing the nuclear button and then saying "my bad." My brother's intent was all clear, though, when I spied our right-hands making their way toward our jet out of the tiny window.

Zeus was seated with his back facing the cockpit and galley, and just as he relaxed his hand and let Ares know the cavalry had arrived, I looked over his shoulder and saw Missy, our flight attendant, heading toward the jet door, stumbling as the fourth gunman jabbed his burner into her back to prod her movement forward. With quiet tears sliding down her face, I could see the fear in her eyes at feeling her last few moments of life slip away.

Right then, it dawned on me that Santiago may have knocked us further off our square than we'd realized. Missy was the second female in the past few months that had gotten caught up in this feud we had going on with Santiago; my brother and I were still fucked up about Cookie being injured in that blast at one of our old traps, so if we made it out of this shit alive, we really had to tighten up.

Santino had just helped us pick this jet out not even a month ago, so I was praying that whatever was about to go down wouldn't fuck it up too much because we hadn't even had a chance to enjoy it. That dude was like family, and knowing that he was gone felt eerily close to the way Pops' death left me feeling several months ago. I felt more than a little fucked up that this shit with Santiago had made Santino's wife a widow before the two of them had gotten a chance to retire on some exotic island and do whatever it was that old people did. A few quick taps from Zeus pulled my attention away from the scene behind him, so I quickly diverted my attention to read his message.

"We need a diversion, just in case," he tapped.

"*Disarm,*" I tapped back. Ares was now clued in as well.

"*On my cue,*" Zeus tapped one last time, and I saw Ares match my nonverbal agreement out the corner of my eye.

"Open it now!" the gunman barked at Missy as she no doubt fumbled to free the door of the jet.

Hearing the release of pressure as the door successfully disengaged, Zeus gave his signal and doubled over in his seat.

"Ahh, shit! Fuuuuck!" Zeus bellowed, leaning forward in what appeared to be agonizing pain. In reality, he was giving himself just enough cover to slide his gun around to his side for quicker access.

Just like he anticipated, Zeus' performance pulled each of the gunmen away from their previous battle stances for a few seconds, but that was all we needed. Like the deadly synchronous force that we were, my brothers and I moved in perfect harmony.

"Fuck off me!" Ares boomed, leaning back in his seat and thrusting himself upward.

Ares' big ass head went crashing into the chin of the nigga that had a gun trained on the back of his head just seconds earlier. Dude's gun slipped from his hand, and Ares sprang into action, snatching it up and proceeding to empty the clip into his assailant's fat, greasy ass body before the weapon even had a chance to come to rest on the floor of the jet's cabin.

In that same moment, Zeus rose to his full height, pulling his piece from his hip in one swift move. A millisecond later, he sent two hot ones into the gut of the dude that had forced him into his seat just minutes earlier.

"What the—" was all that dude behind me was able to get out before Ares made a two for one move and sent a shot ripping through dude's forearm.

I couldn't count the number of times I had cursed Zeus out in my home gym for trying to kill me with that "just one more rep" talk, but times like this made me appreciate the nigga's big brother assertion because I was damn sure about to rock this fuck ass nigga to sleep for messing up my waves.

Dude dropped his gun and snapped his free hand into place to cradle the hole Ares had just torn through his ulnar and radial arteries—bad move on his part. With a good 1,200 pounds per square inch of vigor, I thrust my elbow back and up, shattering the gunman's trachea into what sounded like a million pieces. I could have left well enough alone, but the more I thought about it, these niggas had us in a headspace where, even if only for a split second, we all feared not seeing our family ever again.

Shit, Zo was on the cusp of pushing my nephew into the world, and Po was carrying what I was already hoping would be another little boy to carry on the DiBiasi legacy. For putting all that into jeopardy and making me break a sweat, this nigga was done. Catching the gun in midair that Ares had just tossed to me, I followed his lead and emptied a full clip into the nigga that no longer had to worry about choking to death.

Ares' irrational ass snatched a second burner from his bag and commenced to lighting up the two bodies with a fresh wave of blistering lead.

"Damn nigga, you think you got 'em?" I chuckled.

"Nope, but..."

He let off the last few rounds and brought the gun to rest at his

10

side.

"Oh yeah, them niggas sleep now," Ares announced, satisfied that he'd erased the last breath of life from each man.

Zeus' victim lay motionless on the floor, and the empty look in his eyes confirmed that the two shots Zeus blessed him with were spot on.

"Kill everything moving, huh?" Knowledge chuckled as he and Bones stepped around the bulkhead wall. A shaky Missy was clinging to Knowledge like she'd fall to her feet if he let her go.

"Y'all niggas good? Shit, I know I don't even have to ask that question as long as Ares' grim reaper ass is in the mix, though." Bones frowned as he walked into the cabin area and gave the scene before him a sweeping glance.

Ares stood in the midst of the two gunmen he'd shot, chugging the last few ounces of a bottle of water. That nigga was so unbothered and in his element surrounded by the products of his destruction. The fool part was that as calm as his demeanor was right then, the nigga was still on ten and probably ready to really light some shit up with whatever arsenal he had in his bag.

"Shit!" Zeus snapped, pulling everyone's attention in his direction. "Zo's not answering her phone now, and neither is Po!"

Just like always, Zeus' family was always in the forefront of his thoughts, no matter what fucked up situation we found ourselves in from time to time. Missing the birth of his first son was not even an option, so we needed to make moves like ASAP.

"I'm 'bout to hit Moms up and make sure everything is straight,"

11

Ares spoke up, pulling his phone from his pocket as he finally moved from his spot and headed back toward the rear of the jet where the restroom was located.

"I'll try Po again, too," I added. "What you got for us, though, because we need to get the fuck up outta here?" I turned to face Knowledge as I waited for Po to answer.

When the call rang through to voicemail, I dialed her right back and got the same result. I left her a quick voicemail to hit me back ASAP and followed up with a text letting her know shit got hot, but that we were en route.

"It's all taken care of, boss man," Knowledge reassured just as two more vans pulled up on the tarmac, right alongside the van he and Bones had shown up in.

"The hell?" Ares frowned as he reentered the cabin area.

"Cleanup, transport, and a flight crew. You know how a nigga do." Knowledge beamed, proud of the on-demand backup plan he'd set in motion without me even asking. See what I mean? This nigga was like a mad scientist or some shit with the way he read formulas and knew what we needed before we even had the chance to make a request.

Not even two minutes later, a few dudes from Ares crew stepped their heavy foot asses onto the jet; just like his ass, they had no grace whatsoever in their steps, and it sounded like a full-on cattle stampede as the three linebacker-size dudes squeezed into what was quickly becoming a full house in the limited space of the jet's cabin area. The third and last nigga brought company with him in the form of the fourth gunman that Bones had taken out the minute the jet's door eased open.

Falling right into step, the guys got to work cleaning up the fruits of our murderous labor and within a matter of minutes, you wouldn't even know that a small-scale gun battle had just taken place on the aircraft.

"Ay, special handing on the last one," I called to the last guy as he did a once over to make sure they'd cleaned the jet to our satisfaction. Zeus gave him a firm nod of approval in return. Santino had been good to us, so I owed it to his family to make sure we went above and beyond to properly handle his remains.

"No doubt. Knowledge already put us up on game," the guy returned Zeus' nod before he exited the jet.

"Aight, so we got shit cleaned up, and that's cool and all, but I think there's too much shit goin' on right now for all of us to be off grid. Y'all niggas got some pressing shit to tend to, so how 'bout y'all go on and make that trip. I'mma hang back with Bones and find out who the fuck thought it was open season and shit," Ares asserted. "Hold up, who the hell is gon' fly this muthafucka?" Ares stood with his arms folded across his chest.

"What's my name?" Knowledge lobbed his response.

"Brainiac nigga that make me wanna change all my passwords and PIN numbers every time you step into a room," Ares teased.

"Facts, because you haven't topped your IRA off in a minute," Knowledge rebutted.

"Nigga, stay yo' Jimmy Neutron ass the fuck away from my shit," Ares shot back, laughing because he knew Knowledge was right.

Just then, we heard a fresh set of feet ascending the stairs right before two new faces made their entrance. I recognized the first face as that of a chick that Knowledge kicked it with from time to time. She was a jack of all trades, and it seemed like whatever he needed done, she was always ready and willing to make it happen. She didn't give me cause for pause, though. It was the chick behind her that caught all our attention—everyone except Zeus.

I knew damn well the last thing I needed to be doing was trying to finesse some ass up out of another chick, but damn, mami was thick as fuck and so stacked that she made my dick epileptic for good ninety seconds. I couldn't stop my shit from jumpin', and judging by the look on Ares' face, I wasn't the only one.

"You guys already know Neicy, and this is Cyn," Knowledge put a name to Ms. Thickness.

"She fine as fuck, but what shorty gotta do with flyin' this muthafucka?" Ares countered.

"That's *Captain* Fine as Fuck—as in I'm your new pilot." Cyn smiled, stepping forward and extending her hand in Ares' direction for a handshake. His face lit up, and I knew that he was already having second thoughts about passing on this trip to stay behind in Miami.

"She's the best there is, so relax. You're in good hands, boss man," Knowledge assured.

"Look, I don't care who's fine and who's fuckin—how soon can you get us to Cuba?" Zeus took control. He'd still been unable to reach Zo, and with neither Moms nor Po answering, he was understandably concerned about what was going on with his wife and unborn.

"How soon can we get that door closed?" Cyn winked, turning to take her place in the cockpit.

After passing me a black messenger bag, Knowledge and Bones dapped us all up and exited. Ares hit Zeus and me with brotherly hugs before pulling a nicely wrapped package from his bag.

"Make sure my nephew gets that the minute his lil' ass takes his first breath," Ares instructed. I still couldn't picture anybody calling this fool daddy except maybe the bitches he dug out every other day, but only time would tell if he was truly ready to take that leap into fatherhood.

Neicy closed and secured the jet door while Cyn got the flight paperwork in order. After Cyn ended a brief chat with air traffic control personnel, Neicy advised us all to buckle up and Cyn had us wheels up, leaving Miami and this war with Santiago behind to deal with another day.

Knowledge was like my secret weapon, so I really needed him to stay behind and keep his eyes, ears, cameras, and moles on point so shit in Miami didn't go left with two of us off grid. Bones and Ares would likely join us later, depending on how long we ended up staying out there. If Zo was actually about to give birth, that meant it would definitely be a long trip for Zeus.

Seeing the Miami coastline grow smaller and smaller, I settled into my seat, popped my wireless Beats in, and tried to make sense of everything I had on my plate right now. I'd just narrowly escaped death, only to walk into another inferno by the name of Zipporah Orozco, and her fury didn't have shit on that of the Orozco Seven. Po wasn't too bad on her own, but once she linked up with her sisters? Man, it was game over. Them girls were like a bunch of irrational and emotional females, walking around with Birkin bags full of live grenades—not some shit you wanted to run up on even if they were in good moods, because those mood swings would have them at your throat just because the wind blew too hard.

Moms always said that God looked out for babies and fools, so I wasn't sure how many more fools we'd be before this shit with Santiago was all said and done.

CHAPTER 3

Ares

$\mathcal{S}$antiago's punk ass was getting too close for comfort, so I decided to cancel my trip to Cuba. There was no way that I was going out of the country to leave Santiago to freely fuck up what we had built. With all three of us gone, he would be able to move how he wanted to, and we would have to hear about it. Fuck that! I didn't have a real reason to be in Cuba anyway besides going to see my mama; other than that, there wasn't shit else over there for me.

I left the airport and headed straight home. The first thing I had to do was get out of these bloody ass clothes. I wanted to hit the streets to get the word, but I couldn't walk around looking like I just walked out of a butcher's shop. On my way to the house, I called Marisol but didn't get an answer. I wondered if she knew about her father trying to take my brothers and me out like last year. When she didn't answer my third call, I grew a little concerned. It wasn't like her to not answer my calls; shit, she usually answered before the first ring was complete.

After taking a long, hot shower, I wrapped the towel around myself then sat on the edge of the bed. This shit with Santiago was fucking with me a little because he had gotten too close to us. The fact that the nigga knew that we were leaving and had us cornered bothered the hell out of me. How was he able to get so close? Lately, I had been on some chill shit, so he must've taken that as a sign to make his move. I knew this chill shit that my brothers were on would get us in some shit, and now I had to bring the beast back out. Any nigga that looked like he worked for that nigga Santiago was fuckin' dead.

When I checked my phone, I had five missed calls and two text messages from Tori. Her texts were asking if I was alright, so I pressed the button to call her back. When shit went down in Miami, it hits the streets first. She must've heard about what had just gone down.

"Ares!" she bellowed through the phone. "Baby, is this you?"

"Yeah, it's me."

"Oh my God, are you alright? I heard you were killed."

"Where you hear that?"

"Chasity. She said y'all were in a gunfight, and the Cartel murked y'all."

"Is that right? Well, as you can hear, I am okay, and my brothers are fine too. Don't say anything, though; let muthafuckas think what they want."

"I need to see you, Ares."

"Swing by the crib."

I could hear her smiling through the phone as she said, "Okay, I'll be there in a sec."

I put my phone back on the charger, then stood up to find some fly shit to throw on.

Tori must've been around the corner because I swear she was ringing my doorbell ten minutes later. It was more like forty-five minutes, but time seemed to be on crack today. I pulled the door open to see her standing there in her red, one-piece short set with a blue jean shirt tied around her waist. She looked me up and down as she stepped into the house. After closing the door behind her, I grabbed the arms of her jean shirt to pull her close to me. My mother wasn't here, so I needed someone to console me after what had just gone down.

"I'm glad you're okay," Tori said with concern in her eyes. "Even though you get on my nerves, I don't want to lose you."

"You're not gonna lose me..." I kissed her lips. "So, don't even worry about that."

She smiled, then placed her hands on my cheeks as she drew me in for another kiss. This was the first time since I'd first fucked her that we didn't have to argue when we laid eyes on each other. I already knew what Tori's problem was; she knew the way she'd gotten got me was fucked up, so she always had it in the back of her mind that I was out fucking someone else. Sometimes, that was true, but most of the time when she thought that, I was out working on our next move with my brothers.

I met Tori when I was fuckin' with this chick named Chasity a few months back. Chasity and Tori were friends, but that didn't mean shit to me. From the moment I laid eyes on Tori, I wanted her sexy ass. She had a beautiful face that followed up with a banging ass body. I mean, this bitch could stop traffic in the middle of I-95. My plan wasn't to be a hoe ass nigga and fuck her, but when she kept giving me the eye, I couldn't help myself.

When Tori got up to go to the bathroom, I gave Chasity some weed to roll to distract her. Like a puppy in heat, I followed right behind Tori's ass. I didn't even let her come out before I burst through the door and stuck my tongue down her throat. The next thing I knew, I had Tori's ass on the bathroom sink, pounding her pussy like a raw steak. As disrespectful as it already was, we weren't even trying to mute our moans.

"What the fuck!" Chasity screamed as she stood in the doorway, holding the blunt I had her to roll.

To add insult to injury, my soldiers were lined up and ready to start their march, so I continued my thrust.

"Fuck!" I cried when my semen spilled into the rubber. Out of breath from the best pussy I'd had in years, I looked over at Chasity. "You want next?"

"You sure you have anything left for me?" She smirked.

Chasity already knew not to come at me sideways because I wasn't her man, and she knew how I got down. Yes, it was disrespectful for me to smash her friend in her house, but she should have known better than to have a fine ass breezy chilling with us. Hell, I met her through another chick I was hitting.

"Hell yeah, I got enough to go around."

Shit, after that fire ass pussy from Tori, I didn't even want to fuck Chasity. She had some mediocre ass pussy, but her head was what made me come back for seconds. What did I end up doing? I faked like

I had some business to handle with my brothers, slid Tori my number, and then bounced. That was the end of the Chasity chapter and the beginning of Tori's.

Tori didn't waste any time making herself comfortable in my house. I watched as she pulled food out of the freezer, then looked through the pantry. I guess she called herself getting ready to cook for me. My adrenaline had been pumping so hard that not once had I even thought about eating. I left her in the kitchen doing her thang while I went back upstairs to retrieve my phone.

My face lit up when I saw the missed call from Armani. Even though she was married now, I still wanted to see her before she left Miami. The other night when I ran into her, I couldn't help but to see the fat ass rock that was weighing her finger down. Usually, I was on the prowl to fuck, but honestly, I just wanted to catch up with Armani. Maybe if she confirmed that she was happy with her husband, I would be able to move on and give this love shit with Tori a try. The only bump in the road I foresaw was when Tori found out about Marisol's baby. Speaking of, she still hadn't hit me back.

"Armani." I smiled when she answered. "How are you?"

"I'm good, Ares. Were you busy?"

"I'm never too busy to talk to you."

"How sweet. Listen, I was wondering if you would be available for lunch today."

"I can make that happen. What time you talkin'?"

"Can you meet me in an hour? Same place?"

21

"That's cool with me, I'll see you then."

"Who are you going to see?" Tori asked, startling me. Before I knew it, I had my gun pointed at her. "What the fuck, Ares?" she panicked with her hands raised.

"Don't fuckin' sneak up on me! After the shit that just went down, I almost blew your fuckin' head off!"

To be honest, low key, I had forgotten that she was here that quick. I wasn't used to having females hanging around my house.

"I'm sorry." She lowered her arms. "I just wanted to ask what type of vegetables you want with your steak."

"Put that steak on hold, baby girl. I got shit I need to do."

She looked disappointed about not being able to cook for me. I didn't want to disappoint her, and I didn't want her to be mad right now. She was trying to please me, but I was doing everything to prevent that. There was a possibility that she would be the mother of one of my children, so I had to learn how to do shit differently with her.

"I like loaded mashed potatoes and any green vegetable, but hold off on that until later."

A smile spread across her face. "Okay. I just want to make sure I feed you right."

"Tell you what, make yourself comfortable while I go handle this business. When I get back, I'll eat the steak and veggies, and I'll have you for dessert. How does that sound?"

She was smiling harder than a thief left unsupervised in a jewelry store with all the cases and the register unlocked.

"I can do that."

I rose from the bed, then kissed her before heading out.

Armani was already seated at the table waiting when I walked into the restaurant. Once she saw me strolling her way, she stood from the table, getting her arms ready to embrace me. I ain't gon' lie; I doubled my steps to get to her quickly.

"Ares DiBiasi," Armani sang.

"Armani Perez," I mocked her.

"It is so good to see you again." She smiled, hugging me. "I still can't believe I finally ran into you after all these years."

"The feelin' is mutual, baby. I feel like I done died and gone to heaven."

She laughed as she took her seat. Like a gentleman, I waited until she was seated before I bent my knees to sit. One of the waiters was walking by the table, and he looked up at me. He stopped in his tracks and set the bottle of wine he was holding on the table.

"Good evening, Mr. DiBiasi. Have you been helped yet?"

"Nope, but there's no hurry."

"Here is a bottle of—"

"Nah, fuck that cheap shit. Bring a bottle of Chateau Margaux 2009 Balthazar."

"Coming right up, Mr. DiBiasi."

I nodded, then he grabbed the bottle from the table and rushed off to his previous destination.

"Looks like you're the man around here."

"I am."

"I always knew that you would grow up to be on some boss shit. What are you doing these days anyway?"

"Running half of the city with my brothers, and tryna take over the other half."

"If anyone can do that, you can." She chuckled to herself, then looked at me. "You're Superman."

I had to laugh at that shit myself because I already knew what she was referring to. Before I could respond, our waitress was walking up with our glasses and the bottle of wine. Since Armani brought up the Superman incident, we began to reminisce.

Armani and I met when we were thirteen. She was the new girl at school, so I had to be the first to talk her. For a thirteen-year-old, she had nice sized breasts that captured my attention first. Her face followed next. Then, the way her hair laid down on the back of her neck. She took the seat in front of me, so I looked at her neck and took in her scent for the remainder of the class period. As soon as class was dismissed, I walked right up to her desk. Shit, I wasn't going to risk a nigga catching her on the way out the class. At first, she looked at me like I wasn't the shit that I knew I was. That intrigued me first because most girls were quick to drop to their knees and serve a nigga up under the bleachers.

Against her wishes, I walked her to every class she had that day. Before each class was let out, I made sure to ask if I could go to the bathroom just to make sure I was on time to meet her. After two days of doing that, she finally gave me her phone number. One conversation on the phone, and I had her from that day forth. That was until the night her parents came home early from their family restaurant.

We were lying in the bed, butt ass naked, dozing off from sex when her mother walked through the front door, calling her. I jumped out the bed, slid my briefs on, and then grabbed my clothes. After giving her a quick kiss, I lifted her bedroom window and jumped out like I was Superman. As soon as my feet hit the grass, I heard a gun cock.

"Don't you fuckin' move, nigger!" Mr. Perez boomed.

Knowing that I might die at that moment, I took my chance to swing my arms around to attempt to grab the gun. I did just that and pushed the barrel away from me. Mr. Perez pulled the trigger, sending a bullet right through their front window. I twisted the gun further to the left, tearing it away from his fingers. With the rifle now in my hand, I pointed it toward him. He had his hands held up with fear in his eyes. It took everything in me to not blow his ass through that window. If it weren't for the love I had for Armani, I wouldn't have hesitated. That was what I meant when I said bitches would fuck yo' head up. There was no way in hell that I should've let that moros y cristianos-eating, cigar-licking ass muthafucka go that night—especially after he'd disrespected my father and me by calling me a nigger. I didn't want to mess up shit between Armani and I, so I backed away from him with the gun still pointed in his direction. It wasn't until I jumped in Zeus' car that I was driving that I threw the gun to the ground.

Little did I know, that would be the last time I saw Armani Perez.

When I tried to contact her later, her phone was disconnected. The next day, I got to school early just to see her, but she never showed up. At fifteen, I didn't know how to handle that shit. From then on, my motto had been *break 'em in and throw 'em out.*

"Only God and my father got me out of that situation that night." I laughed. "Hell, that was the first and the last time that I've ever been scared of anything."

"So, tell me what's been going on with you, Ares. I don't see a ring on your finger, but do you have a girl or kids?"

"A chick says that she is pregnant with my seed, so I'll see when it gets here."

"What you mean a chick? Is she not your girlfriend?"

"Nah, that girlfriend shit just don't seem to work out for me."

"Still the playboy type, I see."

"It's your father's fault. If he wouldn't have sent you away, my heart wouldn't have been broken, and I wouldn't be scared to love again. I never loved a girl until I met you."

Armani was my best friend back in the day, so I wasn't going to hold the truth from her. It was actually a relief to finally admit it to someone.

"I hate that for you, Ares, but I want you to find love. It's out there. For obvious reasons, it's not me because I am happily married."

"You know, I've always hated your honesty."

She started laughing, then cut it short when someone approached the table. I looked up to see Tori standing there, steaming like a pot of crab legs.

"Oh yeah, Ares?" she snapped. "You got me at the house cookin' while you're out to eat with another bitch?"

"Sit down, Tori," I said, calmly.

"You got me fucked up!"

I looked her sternly in her eyes and said, "Cause a scene in this muthafucka if you want to, and I'mma turn into Denzel from Training Day on yo' ass. Now, sit the fuck down before I embarrass the fuck outta you, me, and her."

She folded her arms across her chest before taking a seat next to me. I wasn't going say anything to her ass now, but when we got back to the crib, I was gon' check the fuck out of her. She knew better than to be following and popping up on me. I had just warned her about the shit not even an hour ago. She wasn't gon' be satisfied 'til a nigga busted a cap in her ass.

CHAPTER 4

Zeus

My stomach was a ball of nerves as the jet descended onto the runway at José Martí International Airport in Havana, Cuba. I still had not been able to make contact with Zo, my mother, or Po, and neither had Titan. I would never forgive myself if I missed the birth of my son. I had been there for the arrival of both of my daughters, and I did not want to break the tradition.

"The car is already waiting for us," Titan said, pulling me from my thoughts.

"Good. Have you had any luck?" I asked him as we landed with a slight bump. I grimaced a little. This new pilot was going to take some getting used to.

"Nah, but I checked with the hospital, and they haven't come through there. That could be a good sign."

"It could be. Zo labored at home with both of the girls until the very last minute. She could be doing the same with our son."

I did not wait for Neicy or Cyn to open the jet door. I quickly gathered my carry-on bag and exited the jet with Titan hot on my heels. I knew he was just as worried about Po. He did not want her to do anything stupid and kill his seed. I tried to assure him that she would not do anything like that. The Orozco sisters were hot heads, but they were still deeply religious, and Roman Catholics did not condone abortions.

"To the Orozco compound," I instructed our driver as we slid into the back seat of our sleek Town Car. Having money allowed you to skip trivial things like trips through customs.

"I thought Zo was staying with Ma and Abuelo José?" Titan asked as the car pulled away from the curb.

"Come on, man. Zo is home. She is near her sisters. She is going to spend every moment she has up under them."

"True. I just hope Po hasn't gone and did some stupid shit."

"Relax. Even though she acts hardheaded as fuck, Po is probably about to burst at the seams because y'all are having a baby," I assured my younger brother as I watched the Havana scenery pass by.

"You think so?"

"She loves your dirty boxers, nigga. She wouldn't keep fucking with your ass if she didn't."

Titan sat back in deep thought. The rest of the ride to the compound was silent. The Orozcos lived on a fifty-acre property a few miles away from our abuelo's compound.

Santos Orozco was my grandfather's right-hand man before they both retired, which was when our father took over the business. Santos was closer to our father's age and was bred to be our grandfather's most trusted advisor. He had been married to Eníd Orozco for over thirty years and fathered seven of the most beautiful women to ever walk the face of the Earth. He also raised those crazy ass women. I couldn't say that they'd picked it all up from him, because Eníd was just as *loca*.

We were greeted by guards when we pulled up to the compound. Upon recognizing our faces, we were immediately let in, and our driver made his way up the steep, winding driveway. I waited with baited breath until we pulled up to the front of the sprawling estate.

Titan and I stepped out into the warm Havana air. The Orozco Estate was just as immaculate as Abuelo José's mansion. The grounds were covered in different colors of Mariposas, Cuba's national flower. The sweet scent of the flowers could lull you to sleep at any given moment. We both looked up at the large, cream-colored estate and sighed heavily. Behind the heavy iron doors lied our women and their sisters. There was no telling what we were about to walk in on.

"You knock," I told Titan.

"Nah, nigga, you do that shit." He chuckled.

I gathered my nerves and climbed the stairs to the front veranda. There was an ornate door knocker fixed to the front door. I lifted the heavy knocker and knocked three times. I stepped back so that I was standing shoulder to shoulder with Titan. I could hear the lock turning before the door swung open.

"So ... look who decides to show up." Cloryz, Zo and Po's oldest sister, surveyed us as if we were lepers.

"Nice to see you too, Cloro," I said with a smirk.

"Why you always gotta be so stuck up? Dante must not be dicking you down right," Titan teased. He always knew how to get under her skin.

"*Cállate, pendejo.* Bitch ass nigga, I don't know what my sister sees in you," Cloryz said, fighting the smile that was forming on her lips. "Come on. Zo is waiting for you."

Cloryz opened the door wider so that we could come in. She waited until we'd stepped into the foyer before she closed the door. I could hear talking coming from the large kitchen. Like most families, life in the Orozco household was centered in the kitchen. I could hear my wife's loud ass mouth as well as her sisters. They were in their element, speaking rapid-fire Spanish.

"I'm glad to see that you're doing ok," I said as I walked up behind Zo. "You haven't been answering your phone."

"My bad, baby. I left it in the room," Zo said, turning around and throwing her arms around my neck. "You smell like gunpowder."

"We had a few… *issues* getting here. It's handled for now," I quickly added, seeing the relaxed expression fade from Zo's face. "Ares and Bones are back in Miami taking care of it. So what's up with you, ma? I thought you were having my son and shit."

"It was a false alarm," Zo said nonchalantly. "Ya Ya made me some tea, and the contractions went away."

My eyes traveled over to Yael, the middle of the Orozco sisters. Yael was also the only sister who had not inherited their mother's icy gray eyes. Her deep, brown eyes were wide and very seductive. Yael gave me a shy smile before focusing her attention back on the corn that she was shucking with Johanna, the fifth Orozco sister. I focused my attention on everyone in the room and noticed that Ananda and Sofia were also

32

in the kitchen. The stove was full of pots. They were cooking. If I was not mistaken, they were cooking all of Zo's favorite dishes. I guess being the baby of the family had its perks.

"Relax, *hermano*," Ananda said with a smile. She was the free spirit of the bunch. She reminded me a lot of the character Lynn from *Girlfriends*. She even wore her hair in loose dreads like her. Ananda was also Ares' smoke buddy when he came to town. Those two could smoke out all of Cuba in a single session.

"He can't help it. That's his boo. Anyway, I think it's sweet," Sofia said with a wide smile. She was the hopeless romantic in the bunch, but don't let that fool you. She was perhaps one of the most gifted with a knife. Where her sisters were good marksmen with guns, Sofia was a master with the blade. She was definitely on some *Kill Bill* level shit.

"Come; let me talk to you," Zo said with a devious smirk as she pulled me by the hand.

She pulled me through the large house with determination. It didn't take long for me to realize that she was pulling me in the direction of her childhood bedroom. She pulled me into the room with hunger in her eyes and shut the door.

"I've missed you, *papi*," she whispered before she kissed me deeply.

I let my hands roam her ass. Being pregnant with my son had added some extra meat back there, and my wife instantly had my man on brick. Zo's hands were doing some roaming of their own. She quickly found the prize she was looking for in the black jogging pants that I wore.

"I missed him too." She gasped as she slowly dropped to her knees. I was surprised at her agility since she was so far along in her pregnancy.

I inhaled sharply as I felt her warm breath at the tip of my pole. Zo had the best head game, and I was in full anticipation of what she was about to bless me with.

"Who has been down here, Zeus?" Zo asked suddenly. Any sign of lust that was in her voice was instantly gone.

"No one," I lied easily. It had been over a week since I let Titan's maid, Taylor, top me off.

"Your ass is lying. I know you let some *puta* suck your dick!"

"Zo, come on, I haven't stepped out on you since that last time," I said instantly, remembering the last time Zo caught me cheating.

Seven Years Ago

"You keep trying me, Zeus," Zo said as the gun shook in her hand.

I sat still in the bed, careful not to make any sudden moves. Like her sisters, Zo was an excellent shot. I knew that she was not shaking because she was scared. Zo was shaking out of anger. This was not the first time I had been caught with my pants down.

"I-I didn't know he had a girlfriend," Snow, one of my side pieces, stuttered.

"Bullshit, puta! You bitches are always trying to get over on Xiomara. Like you don't know she's with Zeus!" Zo screamed, talking about herself in the third person. I knew then that she was beyond angry.

"Zo, I—"

Zo quickly held her hand up to silence any apology coming from my lips. "Save it," she said with defeat in her eyes.

I watched as she lowered the gun. Her shoulders slumped before exiting the bedroom of the hotel suite I obtained for my rendezvous with Snow.

I had really fucked up with Zo. I could see it in her eyes. I sat back on the bed because I knew I could not go after her with the gun still in her hands. She would shoot my dick off before I could blink.

I was so lost in my thoughts that I did not notice Snow scrambling to put her clothes on. She was shook, and I couldn't blame her. She almost lost her life over some dick. At least it was some damn good dick. I couldn't help but brag; I was slinging some grade A beef.

"We gotta get outta here. Can you take—"

POW!

A shot rang out, causing me to flinch slightly. I watched as Snow's body hit the floor, revealing a seething Zo.

"No, bitch. He can't take you anywhere, but I can send you to hell," she spat before focusing her gaze on me. "Clean this shit up."

I said nothing as I watched her leave the room once again. I reached for my Balenciaga slacks on the floor and fished out my phone to call my clean-up crew.

"Oh, and Zeus?" Zo called out to me.

"Yes, baby?"

"I'm pregnant."

That was the first and only time that my infidelities led to me having to bury a body for Zo. Snow's family still had not had the closure they wanted, and they would never get it.

"Hello!" Zo snapped her fingers in my face impatiently. "Who you been letting slob on your dick, Zeus?"

Zo mushed me in the forehead with her index finger, and I caught her by her wrist.

"What I tell you about your hands?" I asked as I backed her up into the bed.

"Stop. I'm not fucking with you now."

I smirked at her. "You can't tell me what to do with my pussy," I informed her as I pushed her sundress up around her waist and snatched her string bikini underwear from her body.

I positioned myself on my knees so that I was face to face with her freshly waxed pussy. My wife had definitely anticipated my arrival. I could smell her Givenchy body wash as I inhaled her scent. I licked my lips in anticipation before I kissed each of her thighs and then her pearl.

"I'm not fuck—ooooh shit, baby." Zo moaned, forgetting that she was just accusing me of fucking around on her.

I smiled to myself as I quickly brought her to an orgasm. I lapped her juices up like a dog dying of thirst. I ignored her pleas for me to bless her with my dick. I missed drinking from my wife's fountain, so I was going to take full advantage.

"Please, *papi*, I need to feel you in me," Zo begged after her fourth orgasm. I finally relented and stood to my feet, wiping her nectar from my lips.

"Turn on your side," I instructed her as I stroked my manhood to its full length.

Since she was so far along in her pregnancy, I did not want to hurt her. I positioned my body behind hers. At some point, Zo must have freed her breasts from her dress because they were exposed. I kissed her shoulder gently as I slid into her wetness. She fit me like a glove.

Zo let out soft moans as I delivered slow, deliberate strokes while massaging her breasts. Her arms were over her head, gripping the back of my neck. Her position offered a deeper arch in her back, and I started to stroke deeper.

"Shit, Zeus, I'm cumming again," Zo yelped.

I didn't want to be a minute man, but I had not been inside of my wife's sugary walls in weeks. When I felt her explode, I had an explosion of my own, releasing my seeds inside of her. The sheets were soaked.

"Don't ever try to keep my pussy from me," I whispered in her ear and kissed her neck.

"Well, you won't be getting it for about six weeks," she whispered back.

"Why?"

"Because my water just broke."

CHAPTER 5

Titan

*A*fter Zo and Zeus dipped off, I said a silent prayer and willed myself to get ready for the shit that I knew was about to pop off up in the Orozco kitchen. Po had barely even acknowledged my presence since Zeus and I had arrived, and given that everything seemed to be okay and Po wasn't in labor, I figured she was probably ignoring my calls.

Even though I could feel the burning glares of Po's five sisters, I kept my cool and took another sip of what I hoped was just bottled water. The Orozco girls were crazy as fuck, so I didn't put shit past them. Just as I swallowed the last gulp and emptied the bottle, I fucked around and made eye contact with sister #1, and I could see the vein right above her right eyebrow jumping; she was just waiting for the perfect moment to let loose on my ass.

"So, you *do* remember the way here, huh? Because I was starting to think you just might be as dumb as you look," Cloro hissed.

"Nah, you right. The nigga is as dumb as he looks because only a dumb ass nigga would be bold enough to play my sister to the left like some thirsty ass baby mama and come up in here smiling and shit," Johanna chimed in, looking up from the bowl of corn that she was shucking.

"Man—"

"The lies you tell—Po might entertain listening to your shit because she's stuck on stupid in love with your ass, but you're full of shit, and even the baby in Zo's belly can probably see that shit," Ananda added, eyes low as hell. If I had to guess, I'd bet she had just finished some of that killer kush she'd been known to grow.

Ananda's vibe was always so laid back and chill because she stayed lifted most of the time, but she could slice and dice a nigga up without even raising her voice. Meanwhile, Po was still in the same spot where she'd been seated when Zeus and I first walked in, trying to front like she was so deeply engrossed in her iPad. I could see that she was legit gon' let her sisters light into my ass, and I made a note to make her pay for it later that night on the other end of my dick.

"Man, if y'all don't calm your Viper assassin asses down; ain't nobody playin' Po. She knows what the deal is," I retorted, smirking because although they were dead serious in every word they spoke, Po's sisters were funny as hell. Fiercely loyal was an understatement when it came to how the seven of them cut for one another, and I couldn't help but smile, knowing the crazy families my seed was about to be born into; that kid would end up with some wild ass DNA on both sides.

"Nigga, who the fuck do you think you're bassin' up on?" Sofia boomed, crossing the floor and closing the distance between us in the quick second it took me to blink.

Apparently, a quick second was also all the time she needed to flip out her first love: the custom-made Benchmade 63 Balisong that Zo and Po had given her for Christmas last year. No matter where she went, you could rest assured that expensive ass knife was always within arm's reach. I knew Sofia was proficient enough to gut and fillet a man before he even knew he was in her sights, so I chilled on the rebuttal that was hanging off the tip of my tongue.

"Okay, alright, just chill y'all. I got this," Po interrupted, finally deciding to put whatever the fuck had her occupied on chill. In the quick glance, I was able to toss over her shoulder, it looked like she was busy tapping out a message to someone in her Facebook Messenger app. It better not had been a nigga either because I was hoping to be able to leave Cuba this time without adding any more bodies to my count.

"Follow me," Po ordered as she rose to her feet and headed toward the kitchen exit, which led to the west wing of their massive family estate. She tossed Sofia a look and exchanged a silent message that was sufficient for her to return the fancy blade to wherever the hell she kept it stashed—that was a mystery to most people, me included, because she always seemed to whip and flip it out faster than the eye could observe.

I walked a few steps behind Po, simply because I couldn't get a read on her mood at the moment. I wasn't sure if being in the company of her sisters had flipped the switch on her inner savage, so I decided to play it safe and keep my distance until we were alone and behind closed doors. Plus, the view from behind her was lookin' A-1 right about now.

I still wasn't sure how far along Po was, but damn, that ass had already started to spread and was testing the limits of the Under Armour tights she was wearing.

Coming to a stop at the end of the hall, she pulled me into a room that not too many people spent time in: the family library. Well, not too many other people stopped off in this room, but Po and I knew it quite well. Back in the day, the library was the one spot where we were always guaranteed to be able get a nice chunk of privacy before one of Po's sisters came looking for her. Since the walls were reinforced with steel to handle the massive weight of the extensive collection of books, they were nearly soundproof and gave the perfect buffer to snuff out Po's moans as I snuck and got a few quick pumps in back then. In fact, this was the very room where we'd lost our virginity to one another.

"Sit," Po ordered as she crossed the floor and took a seat on the antique, mahogany-caned sofa that flanked a large picture window. It was a gift my grandfather had gifted Po's mother shortly after Po's father, Santos, came aboard as one of the most trusted advisors in our family's organization.

"You ain't gon' cut a nigga, are you?"

"You ain't gon' try to mind-fuck a bitch, are you?" Po sneered, and I could tell she was still heated by how deeply her brow furrowed. Truthfully, we really hadn't had a chance to discuss her pregnancy or how we would move forward, so yeah, she probably had a ton of shit built up that she was about to hit me with.

"Oh, you don't have shit to say now?" Po pressed, folding her arms across her chest.

"Oh, I got a lot to say, but you got it." I threw my hands up in surrender and pressed myself deeper into the sofa, getting comfortable because I knew this wasn't gon' be a short chat.

"Oh, I got it, huh? How can you just sit there like shit's all good, like you don't have a care in the world?"

"Po, sweetheart, look. I need you to relax. I told you I got you, so chill out before you give my seed a migraine," I joked, hoping to lighten the mood.

"Titan, I swear I'm trying my best not to dig my foot off dead in your ass right about now. See, this is the side of you that I absolutely detest. How the fuck is it humanly possible for you to be so selfish? You really think this is all a game, don't you? This is my damn life!"

"Correction—it's our life as soon as you stop playin' like you don't like me. You see the look on my brother's face, knowing his lil' man is about to enter the world? That's the shit I'm tryna be on, but I can't get there if you keep actin' like you want a nigga to be a weekend dad and shit."

"What makes you think you're gonna be a dad? I never said I planned to move forward with this pre—"

"I respect the shit outta your family, Po, but all due respect, I will fuck you up for even thinkin' that shit you almost let come out your mouth. This ain't even up for debate. You *will* have my seed, and you *will* bring your ass home. Ain't shit else to discuss but what we're gon' name his lil' ass. Understand?"

"This is why we always have a problem, Titan, and I promise you that I'm literally two seconds from letting Sofia and her blade have their way with you. You can't talk at me and expect me to just fall in line like you own me or something. That's not how I roll, and you know it. Like I told you before, I am not about to walk around here looking like your long-lost baby mama while you play house with ol' girl. You want alllll the perks of being my dude but don't plan to put in the work that goes along with that."

"The fuck? What are you talkin' about, woman? I been rockin' with you for how many years? And I'm still rockin' with you. I told you what I wanted and where I wanted you. You're the one that keeps shooting me down, so how the fuck am I the one in the wrong?"

"Are you serious? What *you* want? Where *you* want me? What about what the fuck I want, Titan? Does that even matter? Does that shit *ever* cross your mind?"

Po was seething mad at this point, and her respirations were so labored that it looked like her breasts were doing their own version of the Milly Rock. Even thirty-eight-hot, she was still the most beautiful woman I'd ever laid eyes on, and the fact that she was so turnt up let me know just how much love she had for a nigga. She was still carrying my seed, though, so I knew I needed to do my part and minimize her stress so she could make it through her pregnancy and deliver without any complications.

Just that quick, Po's mood shifted, and she went from spitting venom to dropping a boatload of tears. Zeus told me that pregnancy made females even more emotionally unstable, but damn. She was just cursing my ass out!

"C'mere, ma. Don't cry," I coaxed, leaning forward to pull her closer to me. Po wasn't a crybaby type of chick, so I knew that she had to really be going through it in her mind and heart about what this pregnancy meant for both of our lives.

"I got you, ma. That's my word. I got us," I emphasized, bringing my hand up to pat her stomach. I smiled, thinking of how cute she was gon' look once she started showing.

"So, you have me and your girlfriend?" Po mumbled, leaning over to grab a tissue from the end table that sat next to her end of the sofa.

"Ain't no girlfriend. I got one woman, and that's you," I corrected her, tapping her chest with my finger.

Was it a lie? Not completely. Things had been run their course with India and me. I knew I was fucked up for basically keeping her around so I didn't have to come home to an empty house, but I also knew I could never love her or any other woman the way I loved Po. I joked around that I wanted to knock Po up to force her hand into moving to Miami to be with me, but I didn't think it would go down quite like this. I was still wrapping my head around the fact that I was about to be a father, but there was no way I'd let another bitch carry my seed. Po was it for me, and I guess what Mama said was true: *"God gives you what you need when you least expect it."*

"Call her, then."

"Call who?" I puzzled. Just that quick, Po was calm and had collected herself.

"Call ol' girl and tell her what you just told me."

The hell? Po thought she was gon' catch a nigga slippin'—keyword "thought"—but fuck all that. I was a DiBiasi, so I was the one that threw people off their square; not the other way around. Case in point.

"What?" Po frowned as I leaned forward and stared at the portion of the antique area rug that rested just beyond her feet.

Just like I intended, she leaned forward to try to get a look at what had my attention. She returned to her upright and seated position, and I sprang into action. Leaving my spot next to her on the sofa, I stood up and dropped down on one knee, sending Po into a panicked rush of tears.

"Oh my God! Oh my goodness! Wait a minute! What are—"

"Tryin' to bring my family home if you say you'll be my wife."

Withdrawing my hand from my pocket, I flipped the matte black Harry Winston box open and shocked my baby mama with a cushion-cut, five-carat, yellow diamond surrounded by a halo of micropavé diamonds. It was the closest I could get to Po's birthstone in terms of stone choice.

I was just about to deliver my official request for Po's hand in marriage when the door to the library came flying open. Po and I both jumped, and I turned from my kneeling position to see Po's sister, Yael, rushing in with a panicked look on her face.

"It's time! He's coming! Zo's about to have the baby!"

CHAPTER 6

Ares

*A*fter Tori pulled that stunt at lunch, I made her ass sit through an extended lunch with Armani. She sat through two hours of us laughing and catching up on each other's lives with a shitty look on her face. I was trying to be funny by making her stay but, at the same time, show her that nothing was going on between me and Armani. Armani was the last person that she had to worry about, so the fact that I wasn't smashing her should ease Tori's mind for now. We'll see how ignorant she acts once she finds out about Marisol and the baby.

When we exited the restaurant, I switched cars with Tori, then went to go check on Marisol. It had been days since I'd heard from her, and I had a gut feeling that something was wrong. There was no way that she would go this long without answering calls from me. Even when she was pissed off at me, she still answered my calls, so immediately, I began to think the worst. Marisol had already mentioned that Santiago would probably kill her if he found out that she was pregnant with my seed. Shit, to be honest, that could be another reason why he ran up on us at the airport. Whatever was going on with her, I needed to find out about it today.

I drove around Marisol's condo three times before parking in front of someone else's. A car was parked in front of her place, so I knew Santiago had eyes on her. Instead of walking up to her front door, I eased around to the back where the balcony was located. Marisol's balcony was on the second floor, so I had to hit a Jet Li move. I ran and kicked off on the brick wall, then grabbed the railing to pull myself up. After lifted my body up far enough, I jumped over the rails and crept toward the door. I pulled my gun from my waist, the silencer from my pocket, then put my ear to the door to listen as I screwed the silencer on. The only sounds I could hear were coming from the television, so I tapped once on the door with the gun.

More than a few seconds went by with no answer to my tap. I twisted the doorknob and just like that, the bitch opened right up. *How the fuck she gon' have the door unlocked with a war going on?* My niggas knew not to fuck with her, but who knew which one of these knuckle heads would do some stupid shit, thinking they were doing us a favor? The sounds from the television were coming from the bedroom; slowly, I eased my way toward it.

I stood at the bedroom door, watching Marisol sleep like a newborn baby. The only thing I could see was her lips and nose because the rest of her was buried under the covers. It was freezing cold in this bitch. Normally, people woke up when they felt someone watching them, so I waited for a minute to see if she would. Slowly, I strode toward her bed and stood in front of her. Looking at her sexy ass lips made me want to pull my dick out and slip it in between them.

"Marisol," I whispered, shaking her.

She cracked her eyes open, then flinched and threw the covers back when she saw it was me.

"Ares." She smiled. "What are you doing here?"

"What you mean? You're the mother of my seed, and you haven't been answering my calls."

Sadness came over her face. "My father has my cell. I'm so sorry, Ares."

"Sorry for what?"

"The baby...it's gone."

"What you mean it's gone?"

"My father... he had someone to abort the baby last night." She began to cry.

I took a deep breath as I rubbed my hands over my face. Don't get me wrong, I didn't want a baby with Marisol, but I had accepted it, so I was looking forward to being a father in a few months.

"Are you okay?" I questioned.

"No. I wanted my baby—*our* baby."

"I did too. It's alright." I hugged her. "I will take care of it."

"Take care of it, how?"

"Like I take care of shit. I already told you what I would do if something happened to my seed."

"I know you don't like my father, Ares, but I don't want you to kill him. Promise me that you will not kill him."

49

"You know I can't promise you that shit. You as well as your father already know how I handle business, and him fuckin' with my bloodline is a no-no."

"Please, Ares, I'm begging you."

"Yeah." I smirked. "Okay."

She was a damn fool if she believed the words that were spilling from my lips. Santiago was a dead muthafucka in my mind, and I wouldn't stop gunning for him until he was six feet deep. Marisol looked to be about a size four, so I would make sure that I sent her a bad ass black dress to wear to the funeral.

"How did you get in here anyway? Rogelio is at the front door."

"I came through the balcony."

She flashed her beautiful smile at me. I smiled back, but my mind was already plotting on how I was gon' kill this muthafucka Santiago. He killed a part of me, so now I had to return the favor. Instead of killing a part of him, he had to be the one to go, but he wasn't the only one that would fall. A member of his crew would see the barrel of my gun every day until I saw his ass.

"Did you really climb the balcony for me?"

"Of course; you had a nigga worried."

"So, what does this mean for us?"

Again, I rubbed my hands over my face. "I don't know, Marisol. I mean, shit between us is complicated due to who you're connected with, and it always will be. Plus, I've been seein' someone."

"You're always seeing someone; that's nothing new."

"I know, but this is a lil' different. I like her a lil' bit."

"So, you're settling down with one woman?"

"I ain't say all that." We both laughed. "But you know."

"No, I don't know, but whatever."

"I got to get up out of here," I said, standing from the bed. "If you need anything, just let me know, alright?"

"Alright," she agreed as she attempted to sit all the way up.

"Don't get up. I'll let myself out. Get some rest, and I'll call to check on you later."

"Okay."

I leaned over to place a kiss to her frontal lobe, then tucked her back under the cover. She flashed that beautiful smile once more before closing her eyes. On my way out of the bedroom, I pulled the door all the way shut. I already knew what my next step would be, and I didn't want her to hear anything.

My first order of business was to see if Rogelio was still outside of her front door. I wasn't going back out the way that I came in; that was for damn sure. I placed my eye up to the peephole, and sure enough, Rogelio was still standing there. After cocking my gun, I quickly snatched the front door open then popped Rogelio upside his head with it. He fell to the ground, so I drug him inside of the condo and down to Marisol's garage. If he happened to wake up before I got him to the car, I didn't want to have to kill him inside of her condo.

I tied Rogelio up with some rope that I'd found hanging in Marisol's garage. He was still alive, but his ass was unconscious. Instead of pressing the button to lift the garage, I lifted it a quarter of the way up manually, then rolled under the door. The sun was going down, which was even better. Now, no one would be able to see me throwing him in the trunk. Soon as I had that thought, I turned to go back into the garage. I didn't want to put in him in Tori's trunk and risk leaving evidence behind, so I'd put him in his own. After rumbling through his pocket, I removed his keys and phone. With Rogelio's phone in my possession, I now had access to Santiago's entire crew.

Rogelio was now in the trunk of his own car while I drove toward the Santiago estate. His phone was jumping, but since it wasn't Santiago, I didn't bother answering. I knew that sooner or later, he would ring this phone if his crew members were not able to get in contact with Rogelio. My phone rang, interrupting my thoughts. Titan was calling, so I picked right up.

"What's goin' on, bruh?"

"Zo just had the baby."

"Oh, really? Is it a boy for real?"

"Yeah."

"Damn, I hate I missed the birth of my nephew, but it's almost worth it. What's going on with you and Po?"

"She mad at a nigga; you already know."

"Fix that shit, nigga."

"I plan to. What you got goin' on out that way, though?"

"Right now, I got one of Santiago's men in the trunk."

"Bro, you couldn't wait 'til we got back?"

"That muthafucka killed my seed, so nah. I couldn't wait."

"What? Is Marisol okay?"

"Yeah, she's good."

"Well shit, handle yo' business then."

"I will."

"Bet that, call me later and let me know what went down."

"A'ight."

Soon as I hung with Titan, Rogelio's phone began to ring. When I saw that the caller ID read *Jefe*, my insides started doing somersaults. Jefe had to be Santiago, so I didn't hesitate to answer the phone.

"Yo," I sang.

"Rogelio?"

"Nah muthafucka, this ain't no damn Rogelio!"

"Who the fuck is this?"

"Yo' worst fuckin' nightmare!"

Click.

His pussy ass hung up in my face. I laughed to myself as I drove up to the front of the Santiago's estate. It wasn't far from Marisol's place, and that was another reason why I had decided to drive Rogelio's car. I knew that I wouldn't have to walk too far to get back to my ride.

I drove Rogelio's car right up to the gate of the estate to make sure that someone would find him. If I was able to get to his doorstep without problems, I would've walked his ass right up to the front door. I was a fool, but not a damn fool, so I wouldn't dare attempt to walk up there solo with one gun. Once I threw the gear into park, I jumped out and walked to the trunk. I pointed my gun toward the trunk, then pressed the button on the keypad. As soon as the trunk popped open, Rogelio was attempting to jump out but hesitated when he saw the barrel. I looked towards the Santiago's estate, hoping to catch someone watching so that I could hit 'em right in their pupil. If someone was watching, I couldn't see their ass from where I was standing. I reverted my attention back to Rogelio then sent two hot ones through his forehead. Fuck it. I didn't have time to play around with his ass all night. I had to get back home because Tori was probably all in a nigga's shit.

CHAPTER 7

Zeus

*B*aby Apollo was perfect. I could not take my eyes off my first-born son. He was the spitting image of me. His delivery was perhaps the quickest of my and Zo's three children. Apollo came into the world meaning business. He embodied the DiBiasi spirit.

"I would like a chance to hold my baby, Zeus," Zo whined from behind me.

I stood up from the lounge chair that was in the corner of the room and carefully walked over to her. I placed a sleeping Apollo in her arms and smiled. My wife could not have been more beautiful than she was in that moment.

"He looks like you," she pointed out. "He even has your dark eyes."

"This one will be trouble," Enid, Zo's mother, said as she entered the room. She was followed by Zo's doctor, Dr. Edison.

"Thank you for coming on such short notice, Doc," I said, holding out my hand for him to shake.

"It's not a problem, Mr. DiBiasi. Imagine my surprise when two men show up at my door. I thought I was a goner, for sure," Dr. Edison said with a nervous laugh.

I smirked. I sent Bones and Knowledge to pick up the doctor and his family. I made sure that he was on the first thing smoking out of Miami and landing in Cuba.

"No worries, Doc. I trust you followed my associates' request and brought your family."

"I did. Although … my wife found it quite odd that we were told to pack lightly even though we were told to plan to stay for a week."

"Oh, yes … about that," I said, turning back toward the chair I was sitting in. I walked over and picked up a black Hermes briefcase. I set it on the bed and popped it open. I watched as Dr. Edison's eyes grew wide. "I hope this covers the inconvenience my family has caused. This is fifty thousand dollars to cover the cost of your services while here. Of course, he needs documentation stating he was born in Miami. My sister-in-law made sure that your wife and children were taken care of as well."

I sent Sofia over to the Edison's hotel with a Birkin bag for Mrs. Edison that held twenty-five thousand dollars and an additional five thousand dollars each for their three children. They were going to have a blast in Cuba on my tab.

"Of course, Mr. DiBiasi, thank you for your generosity," Dr. Edison said as he focused his attention on Zo and Apollo. He set his doctor's bag on the bed and pulled out his stethoscope. "Let's see what we have here. He looks healthy, and how is mom doing?"

"Fine, Dr. Edison. My mother helped with the delivery," Zo said, nodding over to her mother.

"How do you do, ma'am?" Dr. Edison said. His thick southern accent was blatantly apparent among all the Spanish accents. "Were there any complications during the delivery?"

"None at all. My daughter did very well. There was no tearing, and the after-birth was delivered normally. We have been delivering babies for years, doctor," Enid said with a satisfied smile.

"Thank you. I will need to complete a vaginal exam to make sure everything is healing correctly, but first, let's check out the little one."

Dr. Edison examined and weighed Apollo. His official weight was six pounds and twelve ounces. He measured at twenty-three and a half inches long. He was definitely going to be tall like his father. After Dr. Edison checked out Zo and wrote a prescription for pain medication, I walked him to the door. I thanked him once again, and he let me know that he would be back the next day to administer Apollo's newborn vaccinations. He was having his nurse overnight the materials to him.

As I was about to close the door, Titan and Po walked in. Po was glowing just like Zo was when she was pregnant. The large rock that my brother put on her finger only magnified that glow. I was glad that they were able to sit down and talk things out. India did not take the break up over the phone well. She had been calling Titan back to back. The calls were so frequent that Titan was forced to turn off his phone. He and Po were coming back from getting him a burner phone.

"Yo, you heard from Ares?" Titan asked me with his brow furrowed.

"He called, but I didn't get a chance to answer. What's up?"

"Santiago forced Marisol to have an abortion. Ares killed one of Santiago's men in retaliation."

I sighed, but it wasn't in frustration. I was sad for my brother. Even though he didn't want to admit it, Ares was excited about becoming a father. I could see it in his eyes, and for him to go as far as to kill one of Santiago's men in retaliation proved it. My nigga was hurt.

"I'll call him," I said, closing the front door.

Titan nodded and headed to the kitchen, hand in hand with Po. I watched them until they disappeared before I pulled out my phone to call my baby brother. I needed some privacy, so I stepped out onto the front porch. I waited for him to pick up the phone. He finally picked up after the third ring.

"Yo," he said. I could hear the Hemi in his Dodge Challenger putting in work. Ares was a sucker for American muscle cars.

"You good?" I asked. I really didn't know what to say.

"Yeah. I guess that shit wasn't meant to be. I didn't want to be tied down with a kid like yo' ass anyway," Ares said with a chuckle, but I knew he was just fronting.

"How are things?" I asked, hinting about our current situation with Santiago.

"It's quiet for now, but I don't put shit past Santiago now."

"True," I said as I watched Cloryz's husband, Dante, pull up with my mother and Abuelo José.

I watched as they all climbed out of the car and walked up the stairs of the large porch. Dante dapped me up, and Abuelo José gave me a firm handshake. My mother was the last to climb the steps, and she did not immediately follow Dante or Abuelo into the house. She stood in front of me for a second before holding her arms open for me to hug her. My mother did not give a fuck that I was on the phone. I chuckled a bit before embracing her tightly. My mother was beautiful inside and out. She reminded me of Laurence Fishburne's wife, Gina Torres, who was also a fellow Cubana. Anytime I hugged my mother, I felt a sense of relief like everything was going to be okay.

"Who you laughing at, nigga?" Ares asked.

"Ma just got here," I answered, knowing he was going to want to talk to her.

"Let me talk to Ma," Ares said almost immediately.

"Call her with your own phone."

"Who are you talking to, Zeus?" my mother asked, being nosey. "Let me talk to him," my mother demanded, holding her hand out expectantly. She was still upset with Ares for not making the trip, but she also understood that he stayed behind so we all would have a home to go to.

I sighed and handed over my phone. I knew better than to tell my mother no. She was the real disciplinarian of my parents. Although Frank DiBiasi ran Miami with an iron fist, he had a soft spot when it came to his sons. We could pretty much get anything out of our father. It was our mother who laid the smack down to our asses.

I handed over my phone and walked back into the house. I walked into the kitchen to grab a beer. Dante was already seated at the kitchen island with a *Mayabe* in his hand. I only drank beer when I was in Cuba, and *Mayabe* was the beer of choice for most locals. If you asked me, it tasted a hell of a lot better than the Bud Light and other brands people drank in the States.

"*Oye, mano, que bola?*" Dante said, taking a sip of his beer. "*Felicitaciones.*"

"Thanks, bro. How is business?" I asked.

Dante handled our business on the Cuban end of things. Dante was the calm to Cloryz's fire. He was definitely not a pushover. Most locals referred to him as *El Diablo*. He definitely made Santos and Abuelo José proud. Anytime I talked to them, they were always singing his praises. I figured he had to have been doing something right if our profits were rising and our product was getting better.

"Business is … business. We got a shipment going out tonight. You've never seen it from my end," Dante said, taking another sip of his beer. "You and Titan should come out and see how we do things in Havana."

"Zo will kill me for conducting business while I'm here."

"Come on." Dante chuckled in his thick Spanish accent. "Don't tell me you're scared of those little Orozco women. Trust me; their bark is worse than their bite."

"I think their bite is worse than their bark," Titan interrupted, grabbing a beer from the fridge.

"They have you all shook, *mi hermanos*," Dante said with a chuckle.

We all shared a laugh. Titan and I agreed to go out with Dante to see the shipment off. He was right, we did not really see how business was handled in Cuba. It was time we learned both sides. Abuelo José was not getting any younger, and that would leave more responsibilities for Dante.

I finished chopping it up with the fellas and headed back to the bedroom where Zo was resting. When I walked in, she was sleeping peacefully with her hand draped over Apollo's bassinet. I slipped off my shoes and slid into bed behind Zo.

"I love you," I whispered to her.

"I love you too, papi," she said, interlocking her fingers with mine.

"You love me enough to give me more babies?" I asked, rubbing her soft behind.

"Damn, papi, let me heal up from this one first," she said with a little giggle.

"I'll give you that," I said as I kissed her on the back of the neck before drifting off for a quick nap before I went out with Dante.

CHAPTER 8

Titan

With my handsome nephew making his entrance into the world, my firstborn on the way, and Po finally giving in and deciding to fuck with a nigga for the long haul, life was pretty damn good. Now, if we could just put this shit with Santiago to bed and get the business back to operating smoothly, we all might be able to relax and get back to enjoying our families.

"Yo, you goin' the wrong way, nigga." Zeus caught me just as I was headed toward the rear of the Orozco estate where Po's room was.

"Ten minutes, bruh. I need to handle something right quick," I called over my shoulder.

"Man, that shit can wait until we get back. Po's ass isn't going anywhere. We need to get to this business, nigga," Zeus barked, probably assuming I was trying to slide between Po's thighs right quick, but I had other plans.

Zeus frowned as he checked the time on the Audemars Piguet Jules he'd been gifted the day prior. As was the case with most Cubano men, Santos Orozco was big on family and legacy, so his heart was full of pride at the birth of his first grandson. Zo had been showered in gifts the minute she touched down, so Santos presented Zeus with the watch as a token of his appreciation for helping birth the first male heir of the next generation. Zeus wasn't a flashy nigga, but he loved a good timepiece.

"Ten minutes," I pressed, waving him off as I kept moving.

Po had passed out the night before just as Dr. Edison was wrapping up his visit to check on Zo and Apollo. Good thing too because, apparently, Po was severely dehydrated after a rough bout of morning sickness. Dr. Edison gave her a quick dose of intravenous fluids and ordered her to take it easy the next few days, so I wanted to peek in on her before I left. I also needed to grab my other phone up and make a phone call that I knew I couldn't make from my burner phone.

Easing the bedroom door shut behind myself as I stepped into the room, I saw that the blackout drapes were still pulled shut, which meant Po hadn't been out of bed yet. Since she'd tossed and turned most of the night, I didn't want to disturb her, so after quietly retrieving my main phone from the nightstand, I gave her a quick peck on the cheek and stepped off into the sitting area that was adjacent to Po's bedroom.

As soon as I powered my phone on, I was hit with I don't know how many notifications from missed calls, texts, and alerts from other apps on my phone. Knowledge had the number to the burner I had picked up the other day, so I wasn't worried about missing out on anything business-related. I scrolled through the notifications quickly and found that most of them were from the same person. Shaking my head, I selected the last missed call and waited for the call to connect on the other end. I planned to just wait and deal with this shit when I got back to Miami, but something in my gut told me that if I took that approach, I'd be blindly walking into some shit that would force me to catch another body.

"Really? So, you just play me to the left and act like I never existed? Like the shit we were building meant nothing to you? This is so fucked up of you, Titan!"

Just like I knew she'd be, India was on ten, and she had every right to be. I would've been lying if I said I didn't feel slightly fucked up by ending shit over the phone with her, but the heart wants what the heart wants, and Po was it for me. I figured India would've been a lot more heartbroken if I'd let her ride out my trip to Cuba, thinking we'd just pick up like the happy couple she thought we were when I got back.

"I swear I expected so much more from you, Titan! How hard is it to just be real with me? This isn't some shit that just happened overnight! And for you to be so reckless as to hit another bitch with no protection and knock her ass up? What the fuck, Titan? Why would you do this to us?" India's voice screeched in my ear with a mix of rage and pleading.

"On life, I know shit seems fucked up now, India, but I just needed to let you know what the deal was."

"Bullshit! You wanted to keep me waiting in the wings while you figured out what the fuck you planned to do! Wanted to make sure I curved all the niggas that try to get at me while you walked around here, still pining over a bitch that don't even want your ass! You're full of shit!"

India just kept screaming at a nigga, and I instantly regretted calling her. Her words were rushing out of her mouth so quickly that I could barely decipher what she was saying. I just felt like it was the right thing to do to at least hear her out and let her get it all off her chest. We'd spent enough time together that I came to actually care about her, but it would never hold a flame to what I felt for Po. I felt like I owed India some closure, and since I had convinced Po to return to Miami with me for good, I thought it was best to get a jumpstart on that closure so that none of this shit with India would spill over into what I was planning to build with Po.

"Hellooooooo! Don't get quiet now! You had so much shit to say before! Answer me, Titan! You owe me that at the very least!" India boomed; her voice cracked under the strain she'd been exerting on her vocal chords for the past few minutes. It was clear that she was an emotional wreck as she was now swaying back and forth between cursing me to hell and pleading with me to give us one last shot.

"India—"

"Just one conversation, Titan. That's all I'm asking for. You should be man enough to tell me to my face that we're over," India begged.

I knew the last thing I should've been doing was entertaining a sit-down or anything else with India, especially after the heart-to-heart conversation that Po and I had before she accepted my proposal. She made it very clear she wasn't for the bullshit and that she would pop smoke the first time she was dragged into any bullshit with India or any other bitch from my past. I also knew that I couldn't just cancel India like a Netflix subscription and expect her to go away quietly, so maybe one last sit-down with her would give me a chance to soften the blow and make her feel less like she was being dumped and more like we were just moving in two different directions.

I blew out a long exhale of frustration and spoke what I hoped would put India at ease until I could get back to Miami. Ending the call, I stepped back into the bedroom, slipped my main phone back into the nightstand, and peeked over at Po one last time. She stirred a little in her sleep, but didn't wake up; instead, she stayed in the same position, with her back facing the door. She looked so peaceful and like she was finally getting some relief, and I made a note to have one of her sisters set up an in-home spa treatment to give her a day of pampering.

Pulling the door to Po's room shut as quietly as possible, I headed back toward the front of the house and out to where Zeus and Dante were waiting. As soon as we were out the gate with the house in the rearview, Dante floored the Toyota 4Runner TRD Pro and had us feeling like we were off-road well before he left the main road and ventured off into the dense tropical rainforest.

"Yo, this is some ill shit," I remarked as we stepped into what Dante explained was the epicenter of our Cuban operations. From the outside, the industrial compound looked like a sprawling collection of long-abandoned warehouses and refineries, but once you cleared the vestibule, you were delivered into a setup that had even Zeus in awe, and that nigga was hard to impress.

Like it was all second nature to him, Dante slipped right into business mode and led us on a tour of the expansive operation that my brothers and I really should have taken more time to become acquainted with in the past.

"Ninety percent of the product that arrives here does so in liquid form," Dante began, giving a sweeping motion toward the massive warehouse we were standing in before he led us to what appeared to be a small changing room. There, we slipped into thin, paper coveralls, and surgical masks before venturing further down the hall. We stepped into a room with tables lining each wall and several boxes stacked on top of each table.

"For every ten boxes that are imported for routing to *Centre de Sierra*, two of those end up here," Dante explained, referring to the outdoor recreation company the Orozco family owned. He reached for the closest box on the table to our left, popped it open, and brought out what appeared to be a large spool of climbing rope.

"Each of these is saturated with three keys of pure, uncut product. Hence all this shit, so you don't accidentally inhale any of the airborne residue," Dante continued, nodding at the protective gear that he'd made us don before entering the room.

"So, question: customs is a beast, and I can't remember the last time I heard Abuelo mention a bust. How do we keep this shit off the radar?" I probed. I was impressed with the operation down here and made a note to chop it up with Knowledge about how to improve our Miami operations when I got back.

"By cutting out the middleman. Shit's flown straight from Colombia on military planes, through military air space, and into military facilities. Closest we'll get to a bust is being summoned to turn over flight logs, and that shit is all legit."

"So, if they press and pull a shipment, can they tell the difference between these and the clean spools?" As always, Zeus stood back and silently took in the surroundings and information Dante was giving us. He knew that I'd ask all the right questions and get any info we needed since I was naturally curious.

"Not at first glance. The clean ropes are sprayed with a sealant that makes the ropes last longer, and that sealant leaves the same dusty residue as you'll feel on these." Dante motioned to the boxes behind him.

"And the weight?" I probed.

"A perfect match. The clean ropes use a solid metal spool while the spools used for these are hollow. An identical match down to the ounce."

"So, if they happen to intercept a box of these and test them?" I pressed while Zeus maintained his stoic stance off to my right, but you could tell from his facial expression that he was just as intrigued as I was.

"They'll test negative and sail through inspection. See, the product is cut in a chemical process that breaks it down into two separate compounds, which are never shipped together. The product will test as though it's a placebo until it's reconstituted with the required additive," Dante informed us. I knew from looking through our financials that we had two of the top chemists in South America on our payroll, and that made perfect sense now.

"Reconstitution takes place down the hall in the lab, and once that's complete, the product is ready for shipment, which we'll check out down there." Dante motioned toward an exit that led to another part of the compound. We stopped back by the changing room and disrobed before we headed to the exit.

I was expecting the exit to deliver us to a large hangar similar to where we received and sent off shipments back in Miami, but I got yet another impressing surprise when we stepped into what looked like a small shipping dock—right inside of the building! Of course, there wasn't a plane in sight, but our eyes came to rest on what looked like a submarine. I looked at Zeus and saw an equal level of intrigue as Dante moved about and gave a few quick commands in Spanish to the workers that were in the process of loading product.

"El Fantasma." Dante smiled, gesturing toward the vessel he'd just referred to as a ghost. "Fully submersible and undetectable by radar, sonar, and infrared." Dante's chest swelled with pride as he gave Zeus and me a second to marvel at what was taking place before us.

"How much does that thing hold?" I asked.

"Seven tons of product," Dante beamed.

"Shit!" Zeus and I both remarked in unison.

Locking eyes, my brother and I gave each other a knowing gaze as we quickly read each other's thoughts and gave simple nods of acknowledgement. After doing a quick walkthrough and giving a few more instructions, Dante led us back out the same way we'd entered, and after loading back up into the 4Runner, we headed back to the Orozco estate.

My burner phone started ringing the minute I slipped out of the back seat and closed the door, and I saw that it was Knowledge calling. He was just the nigga I needed to talk to because the shit I just witnessed blew my fuckin' mind! I knew he'd appreciate the high-tech operations we had in place down here just as much as me, so I was excited to pick his brain on how to step our game up in Miami.

"Yo, nigga, I was just—"

"Boss man, we got a problem. Your shit's on fire."

"What the fuck? What you mean my shit's on fire? What shit?" I snapped, and Zeus paused mid-stride on his way up the front stairs. Hearing the alarm in my tone, he turned around and looked at me.

"Your shit as in where you lay your head, boss man. Sheriff's office called when they couldn't reach you. I'm on my way to your spot now," Knowledge assured me, and all I could think about was how this nigga Santiago was gon' keep coming after my brothers and me until we cut that muthafucka's head off. First, he tried to take us all out on our jet. Then, he sent a warning to Ares through Marisol, and now he was coming for my shit. This was definitely a war.

"Fuck, lemme get at Zeus and see how soon we can head back."

"No doubt. One more thing, boss man. I logged into their communications, and it sounds like they recovered a body from your shit as well."

Oh, shit! India!

CHAPTER 9

Ares

*E*ver since that shit went down with Rogelio, Black hadn't left my side. He was pissed at me for not alerting him of what was going down. Shit, at the time, I wasn't thinking about no one; I just handled my business. We both knew that it was only a matter of time before Santiago retaliated, and Black wanted to make sure he was around for the action. Tick and Poody were on patrol with their crews, watching our spots. Someone set fire to Titan's house, so everyone on the payroll was on the lookout somewhere. We were taking every precaution to protect what we had left in case Santiago wanted to blow up some more shit.

I stepped out of the shower, wrapped a towel around myself, then walked into the bedroom. Tori was sitting up in the middle of the bed, eyeballing me. She hadn't left my side since the shooting at the airport, and I was cool with it. A nigga had been eating real good, and sex was on the regular, so I had no complaints about her being around so much. Plus, she kept me company while my entire family was in Cuba.

"Where you goin'?" Tori questioned.

"I gotta pick my brothers up in a lil' bit."

73

"Do you have to go *right* now," she asked, throwing the covers away and exposing her naked body.

"You gon' get a nigga cussed out." I smiled as I traveled toward her.

"You can take it." She giggled.

I dropped my towel, then pulled her by the ankles to the edge of the bed. "You just take this dick."

"Give it to me!"

I kissed her as I rubbed my hand over her clit. She let out a moan through her nose, then softly bit down on my bottom lip. Her pussy was already wet, but I went down to suck on it anyway. I liked for the pussy to be soakin' wet before I beat it down.

"Sss," Tori sucked her teeth. "I want that dick, Ares."

"You gon' get it; just accept this first."

She placed her feet on my shoulders, then pulled my head closer. I spread her pussy lips wider and stuck my tongue as deep as it would go. My tongue was long, so I was able to tickle her G-spot with the tip of it. That shit always drove her ass wild.

Seven inches deep and only ten minutes in, my cell phone started ringing. While continuing my strokes, I reached over onto the nightstand to grab it. When I saw Zeus' name illuminating on the screen, I knew I was late picking them up.

"I'm on my way, bro," I panted.

"Nigga! Get out the pussy and get yo' ass up here!"

"Uhh," I grunted. "I said I'm cummin'!" Tori began to throw her pussy back harder on me. "Shit!"

"Now, muthafucka!"

I didn't respond because I was right there. Zeus continued to curse in my ear; then, Black knocked on the bedroom door. I thrust a few more times before pulling out and squirting my seeds on her stomach. Once I realized that I was still listening to Zeus curse in my ear, I hung up the phone in his face. I already knew what would come from him when I decided to slide in Tori, but the shit was well worth it.

After throwing my clothes on, I jumped in the Charger and took off. Black was in his Mustang behind me, weaving in and out of traffic as he tried to keep up. I had the pedal to the metal, and I wasn't letting up for nothing. Zeus was probably boiling hot by now, but I thought they were landing at ten. I must've miscalculated the landing time, or they had left earlier than planned. Whatever happened, I would surely hear about it the entire ride home.

As I drove up, I laughed inside while looking at Zeus' tight-lipped ass. I swore he looked just like I'd imagined he would: all frowns with steam coming out of his nose like a damn dragon. Titan looked like he had shit on his brain because his facial expression was blank.

"When you start puttin' pussy first?" Titan questioned as soon as he opened his door.

"Bro, I thought I had another hour, no lie. How Zo and Apollo doin'?" I asked Zeus when he slid into the backseat.

"They good," Zeus replied dryly.

"My bad, nigga. I thought y'all was gon' be here at ten."

"We left early, and you would have known that if you had checked your text messages."

Right then, I unlocked my phone and went to my messages. I had one from Zeus, one from Armani, and one from an unknown number. Since I already knew what Zeus' message said, I opened the one from unknown number first.

305-555-1983: Ares, this is Mari. My father's gonna send some1 after u 2day for wht hppnd 2 Rogelio. Plz wtch ur bck.

I looked over at Titan, and he looked back at me with questioning eyes. My brothers knew me, so they could always tell when something was wrong. I dropped the phone back into cup holder, looked around the lot, and then mashed the gas.

"What's up, A?" Titan finally asked.

"That nigga Santiago is sendin' someone for me today over that Rogelio shit."

"Shit, we already knew that. Why you look shook?"

"I need to get Tori out of my house. I don't want nothin' to happen to her behind this shit."

"Well, you need to let her know what's up."

POP! POP! POP!

The sounds of gunshots rang out, and bullets began to rain against the driver side of the car. Good thing my shit was bulletproof, or I would've been a dead muthafucka. I looked in the rearview mirror and saw Black's arm out his window, already blastin' at them fools. I reached over to pull the glove compartment open so that Titan could get the gun.

"Showtime!" Titan announced, then jumped in the backseat with Zeus.

"Grab that gauge from under the backseat," I barked at Zeus.

The back window eased down, causing my ears to pop, then shots went off behind my head. That shit seemed louder than it ever had in the past. My ears were on fire. When the car tried to speed away, I mashed on the gas to keep up. These muthafuckas weren't gonna get away—not after trying to assassinate my brothers and me. Fuck no! My plan was to kill everyone that Santiago sent our way until he showed his bitch ass face. If I had to murder a thousand muthafuckas to make him show up, then that was exactly what I would do. That man would have to face me sooner or later, and when he did, I was gon' shoot his face into the back of his skull.

As we drove down the freeway exchanging gun fire, other cars were gettin' the fuck out the way. We were all driving recklessly, so I didn't blame them for pulling over. I didn't always give a fuck about murkin' no niggas, but I hoped no innocent people got shot behind this shit.

"Man, y'all can't hit them bastards!?"

"If you stop drivin' like a maniac," Zeus shot back.

"Hit the driver!"

Titan let off two shots, and the car started to slow down before veering off to the right across the expressway. I watched as it came to a complete stop after hitting the guardrail. I pulled in front of the car and jumped out. My brothers were right behind me, and Black was coming from behind their car. We all had our guns drawn as we eased toward the windows. Every nigga in the car was leaned over the seats. Black pulled the car door open, then began to shoot each one of them in their heads.

Black took all the guns and went one way while we jumped back into the Charger and headed to Titan's house. He wanted to see the damage that was left behind by the fire. I knew that he would be pissed because I was pissed when I saw it. They hadn't identified the female that was killed in his house yet, so he was on edge about that. He was probably thinking the same shit that I was: India.

When I pulled up to Titan's house, he and Zeus jumped out. I grabbed my phone to call Tori. I needed her to get away from my house, especially after what had just gone down. Sooner or later, Santiago might try to blow up my shit.

"Hello." Tori smiled through the phone.

"Yo, where you at?"

"Yo' house."

"I need you to get yo' stuff and go home."

"What?!" she asked, sounding offended.

"Not like that. Some shit just went down, and I don't need you at my house. It might not be safe there for you. Go home. I'll come by when I finish with my brothers."

"Ares, what's goin' on?"

"We'll talk about it later. Right now, I need you to get out of there. Leave your car there and take the Audi."

"Why?"

"We'll talk about it later! Damn! Just do what the fuck I'm tellin' yo' ass to do! I done told you 'bout askin' me so many fuckin' questions."

"Don't yell at me, Ares!" she whined. "I'm just tryin' to find out what's goin' on."

I let out a deep breath. "Are you fuckin' listenin' to me or what? Did you hear what I said?"

"Yes!"

"Well, do the shit!" I yelled before hanging up the phone.

I already knew that her ignant ass was gon' call back, so I turned the ringer off. She was gon' make a nigga knock her fuckin' teeth out one day, asking me a million questions. I couldn't stand a hard-headed bitch, and Tori's sexy ass was just that. She better be glad she had that killa pussy and bad ass body, or I would've been tossed her ass out like yesterday's trash.

"What we gon' do, bro?" I asked as I walked up behind Titan.

"I need to wrap my mind around all this shit. Too much is goin' on, and I haven't had time to think. But on the real, I don't think Santiago did this. He knew that we were out of the country, but Ares was here. Why would he blow up my spot and not Ares shit? Nobody's shit was touched but mine."

"So, what you thinkin'?"

"Iono yet. I need some time to process this shit."

"Don't you have yo' cameras backed up at yo' condo?" Zeus asked Titan.

He wrinkled his eyebrows. "You know what? I think I do."

"Shit, well let's go check 'em out."

"Let me call Knowledge; he knows how to pull all that shit." We all started back toward my car. "Plus, we need to talk about our operation."

"What about it?"

"Oh, man," Zeus boasted when we got in the car. "The operation in Cuba so damn sexy it made my dick hard."

"Damn, like that?"

"The shit is impressive, I'll tell you that. If we can get shit like that here, won't nobody ever be able to fuck with us."

"You got a nigga wantin' to see that shit."

"In due time, baby brother." He smiled. "In due time."

CHAPTER 10

Zeus

*S*hit with Santiago was getting out of hand. We'd just had a high-speed shootout down the interstate in broad daylight. That nigga clearly had a death wish, and I was about to be the one to sign the death certificate. I knew I needed backup. Although my brothers and I had a strong army in Miami, we needed more.

I played with my phone in my hand. I knew once I dialed the number, we would be journeying down a rabbit hole. I was not left with much of a choice. Santiago needed to be dealt with. If anyone could deal with him, the mob could get the job done. I took a deep sigh before I dialed the number.

"Hello," he answered on the second ring.

Here goes nothing, I thought before I opened my mouth to speak.

"Vincent?"

"Yeah. Who is this?" he said in his heavy, New York accent.

"Zeus," I said as my eyebrows furrowed in frustration.

"Get the fuck outta here. Cousin? You slumming it now?"

"Don't do that, Vinny."

I immediately started to regret my decision in bringing my father's side of the family into things. Frank DiBiasi was a full-blooded Italian. His father, Dominic, rose through the ranks of the Gambino crime family along with his brother, Nicholas. My cousin, Vinny, was Nicholas's oldest son and a royal pain in my ass.

Vinny was not as business-minded as me or Titan. He was a hothead like Ares. He wanted a taste of what we had going on in Cuba, but I was always wary of bringing him into the fold. His brother, Anthony, handled my financial holdings, but that was about the gist of how involved my father's side of the family was in our drug trade. Italians were notorious for laundering money, and Anthony was the best in the business in our generation.

"What do you need handled?" I could hear the smile in Vinny's voice.

"I just need back up." I ran my hands over my face, hoping that I was not making a big mistake in calling the DiBiasi clan for reinforcement.

"Say no more, cousin. We're on the next flight out."

"Vin?"

"Yeah?"

"We need heavy artillery. This thing is bigger than I anticipated," I admitted. I hated to admit that I was wrong in any situation.

"Understood. Don't worry about it," Vinny said in his heavy, Staten Island accent.

I hung up the phone and let out a deep breath. I knew once Ares and Vinny got together, there would be maximum carnage throughout Miami. They were like Kane and the Undertaker from WWE. They were the proverbial Brothers of Destruction. Vinny was, by far, Ares' favorite cousin. They both killed without remorse. I knew that he would be happy to hear that Vinny was coming to Miami, but I could already imagine Titan's face. I knew he would think that we would risk bringing unnecessary attention to ourselves, but I wanted Santiago handled. I wanted my family back in the States with me.

Since Vinny said that he would be on the next flight out, I needed to let my brothers know of the plans moving forward. I saw that handling Santiago in a civilized manner was not winning the war. It was time to just wipe them out completely.

Luckily for me, Titan was staying in my guest house since his house burned down, so I did not have to go far to deliver the news. I backed away from my desk and stood up from my chair. I felt like I was walking to deliver bad news; I guess I was doing that in a sense. If people thought that Ares and the Orozco sisters were loose cannons, they hadn't seen the full potential of the crazy ass Italian side of our family. Italians were notorious for being hot-tempered.

I crossed my large foyer and walked through the kitchen until I reached the French doors that led out to the pool area. We had an Olympic-size infinity pool that overlooked the marina that we lived on. I had a mini-yacht stationed at the dock that we would take out from time to time and relax. Zo and I had a larger yacht over at the yacht club where my brothers and I usually met.

"Fuck you going?" Titan asked from the hammock on the far end of the pool.

"Shit, I was coming to see you. I got some news."

"I already know Santiago burnt my shit down."

"Not that. I called in reinforcements," I said, taking a seat on the lounge chair so that he couldn't see my face.

"Why would we need reinforcements? Who did you call?"

"Shit nigga, you want to have another dead body from our team? I called Vinny. Let them muthafuckas get in the dog fight."

"So, you called Vinny's crazy ass? Ain't it bad enough we gotta keep Ares on a leash? Now, we gotta worry about Vinny's crazy ass too?"

"Ain't nobody got me on a fucking leash," Ares said out of nowhere. "Shit, let Vinny bring his ass down here so we can wreck some shit."

"Fuck you come from?" I asked. I was relieved that at least one of my brothers was on board with me calling our Italian relatives for backup.

"Ana let me in. I just came from checking on Tori. I sent her ass back to her own shit."

"Damn, I can't just picture you shacking up with one bitch," I commented.

"I ain't. That pussy just too good to stop fucking with. Tori know what the deal is." Ares shrugged.

"Yo' ass better be careful before you have a fatal attraction on your hands. These hoes don't be playing," Titan added, sitting up in the hammock. His phone started ringing, so he stepped away from our conversation.

"So, what's up, lil' bro? You feeling Tori enough to make her your main?" I asked Ares as he took a seat on the lounge chair that was next to me. Ana did not miss a beat as she set a tray on the table between us. It had a bottle of Louis XIII and three glasses of ice.

"Man, I'm not saying all of that, but it does feel nice to have in-house pussy I can slide up in whenever I need to," Ares replied, running his hands through his hair.

"I just hope you wrapping up when you sliding up in these hoes. You gon' fuck around and get something you can't get rid of or worse; your dick is gon' fall off," I said with a chuckle.

"Man, I been letting Tori wet my dick up."

"Aight nigga, you 'bout to fuck up and have another seed on the way. You know we fucking fertile. We got that super sperm."

Ares and I shared a laugh as I stood up to pour us both a drink. My phone vibrated in my lap, and it was Bones letting me know that he had landed in Cuba. I told him to meet with Dante so he could also get a glimpse of the operation in Cuba. He confirmed that Dante picked him up from the airport, and they were en route. He also said he was putting another baby up in his wife while he was down there. I chuckled as I went back to pouring drinks. I caught a glimpse of Titan heading back to us, and he had a worried expression on his face. I stood straight up and watched him try to make another call, only to hang up immediately. He tried two more times before letting out a frustrated sigh.

"What's wrong?" I asked.

"The body they found wasn't India. It was Taylor," he answered as he slumped into a nearby lounge chair.

"Well, where is India?" Ares asked.

"I don't know. She isn't answering her phone, and they haven't seen her at the shop in a few days," Titan said with stress lacing his voice.

"This shit reeks of Santiago," I said before guzzling my drink and pouring another one.

"If that's how he wants to play it, let's play," Ares said with finality. Titan nodded his head in agreement before turning his drink up.

CHAPTER 11

Titan

"*N*igga, where the fuck you gotta go all of a sudden? We got shit to tend to," Ares mumbled like he had woke up on the wrong side of the bed. Truthfully, that was exactly what happened since we all ended up crashing at Zeus' crib last night.

"I said I'm not gon' be gone long. I gotta make a run and handle some shit right quick."

"And we need to lay this shit out right quick so we can be ready to get it in when that nigga Vinny touches down."

Ares was talking to my back now since I was just a few steps away from the door leading out to Zeus' garage.

"Man, don't have us waitin' on yo' ass all fuckin' day. You ain't the only one that got shit to do—"

"Gotdamn nigga, I heard you the first time. Shit! Yeah, lemme make this shit quick so you can go let Tori fuck yo' ass into a better mood."

Ares was still bitchin' when I shut the door, but I didn't pay that fool no mind; I had already planned to step out and handle a few things alone this morning, and I didn't need his fuckin' approval. That nigga was just salty because he didn't get to sleep up under Tori's ass last night like he had planned to.

I mashed the button on the wall to let Zeus' garage door up, and of course, Ares had parked behind me and blocked my shit in. I swear it felt like this nigga was about to be a thorn in my side today, and I had too much shit on my dome to be beefin' with him. There were plenty of niggas in the streets for me to project my anger on; I just needed the chance to get my hands on 'em. I wasn't trying to go back inside and get into it with Ares for real—because that nigga didn't fight fair—so I just grabbed an extra set of keys I knew Zeus kept in his lock box and took one of his rides. I figured Zo's Range Rover hadn't been driven in a minute since she'd been in Cuba for a while, and once she saw the push present Zeus planned to surprise her with—an Alfa Romeo Stelvio—she wouldn't give two fucks about the Range. My big brother had some serious connections because that shit wasn't even available for purchase to the public, yet he had managed to snag one fresh off the assembly line. I smiled to myself, thinking of how my brother held his family down with every breath in his body, and I figured that if I could be even half the husband and father he was, I'd be able to keep my promise to Po and my unborn.

ME: took Zo's truck, be back in a min

Z: no prob, make that shit quick

After adjusting the seat and mirrors from the programmed settings for Zo's lil' ass, I whipped out of Zeus' driveway and hit the highway. My original plan was to go tend to the shit concerning Taylor, but I decided to make another stop first to go on and get it out the way. Not too long after I'd merged onto the exit that I knew like the back of my hand, I was cruising the streets that were intimately familiar to me. I needed to see it for myself and without the animated reactions from the peanut gallery—AKA Ares. Zeus probably woulda been cool, but I knew seeing this shit would only put Ares' ass on ten, and that nigga was hyped enough as it was, looking forward to fucking some shit up with our cousin, Vinny.

I decided to park on the curb and walk up, so I slid through the gate and trudged up the long driveway to see what was left of my house. Knowledge had swung by to check out the damage for himself and even took some pictures to send to my phone, but nothing prepared me for the shit I walked up on. The house appeared to be intact from a distance, but the closer I got, the more I could see how fucked up it was. Half of my house had literally burned to the ground, while the other half stood there, looking less like the structure I had called home for some years, and more like half of a dollhouse. This shit was definitely a total loss, and even though I was looking forward to a new beginning in a new place with Po, standing here looking at what was left of my house tugged at a nigga's heart.

A part of me was glad that the body they pulled out wasn't India's, but I felt even more fucked up that it was Taylor, my part-time maid. As far as I knew, she had no family, which was the reason I was headed to pick up her ashes as the most logical next of kin. My brothers didn't know this, but I met Taylor a few years back when I made a run with a nigga I'd gone to college with. He was swinging by his old frat house to show some love to his line brothers, and he swore that their parties always brought out the baddest bitches. Of course, I had to see for myself, so I was down to slide through and make it a night to remember. I also remembered that was the night Po cussed a nigga out so bad that I was afraid to call her for a whole week. I didn't even remember what I had done, but whatever it was, she'd had enough on that particular night.

I only caught a side view of Taylor at that party, mainly because she was so lit that she danced nonstop the whole time we were there and with wall-to-wall people, so that was the best view I was gonna get. Fast forward a week later and while making a run to grab some Aleve for a headache I couldn't shake, I saw two niggas coaxing a very drunk Taylor out of a bar and into their van. She looked barely conscious, as they were actually moving one leg in front of the other for her. I wasn't the type to be on no captain-save-a-hoe shit, but the decent nigga my mama raised me to be wouldn't allow me to just sit there and watch that shit go down. All I could think was that someday, my nieces would be college girls just like Taylor, and I'd take out a whole fuckin' country if I even thought some niggas tried to take advantage of them like those niggas had planned to do with Taylor.

After running the niggas off and taking Taylor back to my spot—Po was supposed to fly in and had cancelled at the last minute—I quickly found out that Taylor wasn't drunk. She was drugged. I had no way of knowing what the fuck they gave her, but it fucked me up watching her go through withdrawal as her body came down off the drugs. Never had I ever seen any shit like that in my life, and after damn near a week of watching her crash, too out of it to even wipe her own ass, she recovered and ran down how she had no family and nowhere to go. She mostly hung out at those parties to con her way into the next nigga's pockets that would slide her a few bills to keep a roof over her head.

Normally, I woulda tossed a chick out on her ass for admitting that her intent was to finesse her way into a nigga's pockets, but Taylor gave me something else in addition to a rundown of her scandalous ways: genuine gratitude. She cried and thanked me over and over again for saving her life, said she took the whole situation as a wake-up call, and pledged her undying commitment to repaying me for putting my life on hold for a week to tend to her when I could have left her for dead. I told her that she could repay me by getting her shit together, and after helping her get enrolled in a local community college to work toward becoming a nurse, I gave her a part-time job looking after my spot. Aside from the fact that I really did need some help keeping my spot neat since I stayed on the go so much, it gave me a chance to lay eyes on her on a regular basis and make sure that she was okay.

Now, Taylor was the second chick to get caught up in this war that Santiago had lured us into, and that shit had my dome feelin' heavy as hell with guilt. Cookie was lucky that she didn't die, but she'd never be the same as she was before the fire she was injured in at one of our traps.

"Man, we gotta dead this shit ASAP. Fuck all this," I mumbled to myself as I took one last look at what was left of my home then headed back to Zo's Range to slide by the funeral home and sign for Taylor's ashes.

Ж

"Yo, I was just about to call you, ma. Everything straight?"

"Yeah, I guess... I'm just sad that you're gon' miss out on this, but I understand," Po pouted into the camera, flashing those sad, puppy dog eyes that made a nigga wanna give her the world.

Po was scheduled to have a sonogram today, and of course, she was disappointed that I wasn't there to go with her to the appointment. I told her to FaceTime me when she got into the examination room so I could get a view of my seed long distance, and I think I was probably more excited than her to see my masterpiece. I loved my nieces and nephew like they were my own; had changed their diapers and everything, but it felt different. Knowing something that Po and I had created was on its way made a nigga's chest swell with pride and shit, and I couldn't wait to see what my lil 'man looked like. Yes, lil' man. I already told Po it was gon' be a boy, and that she could get all that mini-me shit outta her head. Mini-me alright—as in a mini version of his pops.

"Okay mom and dad, here we go..."

I was sitting in the Range, waiting for Knowledge to show up, and not even a full minute later, my unborn's figure populated the monitor. My lil' man was floating around like he didn't have a care in the world, and I felt a few tears pool in my eyes as I was seeing my firstborn for the first time.

"So, here's a leg, mom and dad... oop, and it looks like baby is a thumb sucker; can you see that right there?"

Po squealed like a kid in a candy factory as she watched our baby on the monitor. The doctor fell quiet while taking some measurements, then spoke again just as Po winked and blew me a kiss.

"Mom and dad, do you want to know what you have cooking in here?"

My eyes lit up with excitement because I just knew I was about to win the lil' bet that I made with Po regarding the gender of our baby-to-be.

"Yes and no. We're planning to have a gender reveal party to share the news with our family, so can you seal it in an envelope for now?" Po tossed a big ass Kool-Aid smile in my direction, knowing she was foul as fuck.

The hell? Why the fuck did I have to wait?

"Ahh, how sweet! And no problem, I can definitely do that for you. Just give me a minute to print a few pictures off and have my nurse package them for you, and I'll have you out of here and on your way, Ms. Orozco."

Ms. Orozco? Not for long. I had mad love for Po's family, but I couldn't wait to make her the next Mrs. DiBiasi.

"Aww hell naw, bruh, please tell me y'all not bonin' on the phone and shit!"

I didn't see or hear Knowledge pull up, but he was now leaning through the passenger window with his face turned up in disgust.

"What's good, nigga? And hell nah, not out in the open like this." I dapped him up before shifting my attention back to Po. "Bae, lemme get up off here so I can check into some things. I'll hit you when I'm done though, aight?"

"Actually, I'll just text you later. Cloro wants to take me shopping for some things for the baby's nursery later."

Here we go with this shit again.

"Long as you make sure you can ship whatever you get back home."

"I am home, Titan. Look, I don't wanna do this right now. I'll just text you later, okay? Love you."

Po disconnected our video call before I had a chance to reply, no doubt purposely, because she knew I was about to get in her ass. My house burning to the ground couldn't have happened at a worse time because I had literally just convinced Po to permanently relocate to Miami. I wanted today to be the last time I missed one of her appointments, and I wanted to be able to spoil her during her pregnancy. I couldn't do that with a piece of ocean separating us.

"You done bein' all in love, nigga? If so, I got some shit to show you," Knowledge joked as I followed him up the stairs and into his place.

"I'mma see if you still talk that shit when yo' ass fall in love. So, please tell me you got good news because a nigga done had enough bad news to last a fuckin' lifetime."

"Depends on how you look it, but I definitely got some answers for you," Knowledge confirmed. "You remember Cyn?" Knowledge nodded toward Cyn, the pilot that made sure my brothers and I made it to Cuba in time for Apollo's birth. She met my eyes with a flirtatious wink, then went back to whatever had her attention on the computer monitor in front of her.

"Sup, girl. So, what you got for me?" I turned to Knowledge, lowering myself into one of the expensive ass chairs that Knowledge had in his conference room. This nigga really did live and breathe his job because although this was a residential building we were standing in, Knowledge had it laid out like a fully functional office/IT department. Aside from the few rooms that were set up for his personal use, it could have easily been mistaken for an upscale office suite.

"This."

Knowledge cued up the footage he was able to recover from my surveillance system; the first few seconds were just snow, but a fuzzy image of my house popped up at the eighteen-second mark. The view jumped from one camera to another, giving me a 360-degree view of the perimeter of my house. When the view switched back to the camera covering the entrance to the maid's quarters at the rear of the house, I could see a fuzzy figure walk right into the frame and up the path to an entrance that was rarely used. Even when Taylor used to swing by, she always used the front or side entrance.

"Can you enhance that?"

"Already on it."

This is why the nigga Knowledge was my ace. I don't give a fuck how hopeless some shit was; he could find a way to make something out of nothing when it came to any and everything related to technology.

Sure enough, he was able to isolate the frame and enhance the image to give us a clear view of whoever the fuck was walking up to my house like they lived there and shit.

"That definitely ain't one of Santiago's men..."

"No doubt," I agreed with Knowledge, confirming my gut instinct. What I was seeing only confirmed my initial gut feeling that Santiago wasn't behind my shit being set on fire. If he was gonna make a move like that, he would've made sure all three of our spots burned to the ground; better yet, them shits woulda been leveled in some well-executed explosions that made the evening news.

"Too tall to be Taylor; plus, she wouldn't be dressed in all black like the omen and shit," I mumbled.

What I was seeing left me with a new dilemma: figuring out who else we had to add to our hit list. Lord knows we had enough niggas to worry about since this shit kicked off with Santiago; now, I had to break the news to my brothers that we might have a new adversary.

"Good lookin' out. Keep workin' on that and see what else you can shake out. I need to know who the fuck ran up in my shit. Oh, I need to get at you about that other shit too, so lemme know when you got a minute to step out to the site."

I was still blown away with the operations Dante showed us in Cuba, and I was eager to get something similar going here in Miami. What we saw was some next-level shit that would put us in a position to have the whole fuckin' country on lock.

Seeing Knowledge go right to work on the video, I figured I'd dip out and let him do his thing.

"Aight, Cyn. Good seeing you again."

"It's always good seeing you, Titan. Alwayssss," she drew the last word out to make it crystal clear she was flirting with a nigga.

Let me get the hell up outta here before Po has a reason to take a nigga's head off.

Ж

"And you still ain't been able to get up with India?"

"Nah bruh, and I don't know whether to be worried or suspicious. She loves them lil' shops more than anything, so I can't see her just up and leaving and not letting someone know she's leaving."

"Unless she don't want to be found," Zeus suggested.

"Shit, you might be right. All I know is two chicks gettin' caught in our crossfire is too damn many."

Taylor's death was really fucking with my head, so Zeus and I were on our way to check on Cookie. Now, it was funny that Ares was pressin' me about goin' off to run my errands earlier, but now this nigga was too busy to roll with us to check on Cookie. I heard him mention Marisol's name on the tail end of his phone call, so I hoped that nigga wasn't tryin' to go off by himself and set no shit in motion to retaliate against Santiago. Zeus made him promise not to make any moves until Vinny touched down so we could all move as a unit, but I didn't have a whole lot of faith in that nigga's ability to exercise restraint, especially after them fools rode down on us the other day.

"Lemme ask you something, Z. How you do this shit?"

"Whatchu mean?" Zeus hit the brakes as we rolled up to a stoplight.

"This, the business, what we do. We can have niggas shootin' at us on any given day, niggas' lives stay on the line, so how you do this shit knowing you got the kids and Zo at home?"

"Simple. A nigga gotta do what he gotta do. You know just as well as I do that we were born into this shit. It's in our blood, so it's not like it's an option or some shit," Zeus explained, merging onto the highway and heading to Cookie's side of town.

"Nigga, I get that. I'm just sayin', shit feels different now. I'mma give Po and my seed the world, that's my word, but I just keep wonderin'... what the fuck is gon' happen if a nigga don't make it back one night?"

"Shit's simple, bruh. When we out there, we gotta have tunnel vision in a sense. Not to the point where you're blind to the shit goin' on around you, but to the point where you so focused on ya goal that you leave no room for error. Feel me? When I'm out there, I ain't stressin' over no bitches, no snake niggas, none of that shit. I'm out there to make sure we get this money, make sure our product is movin', and we take our asses home at the end of the day.

"I feel you." I nodded, taking in everything my big brother was spittin'. Zeus had a lot of responsibility to carry on his shoulders, and it had always been that way. He went right from lookin' out for me and Ares to havin' a family and making sure they were good. He always wore that hat of accountability, so shit, if I had to learn how to juggle all the shit I was about to have on my plate, he was the perfect example for me to follow.

"At the end of the day, I know I better make it home by any means necessary. Otherwise, Zo will resuscitate my ass just to kill me again for makin' her a widow and leavin' her to raise a bunch of kids alone." Zeus chuckled. That sounded like some shit Zo would do too.

"Man, you know Po trippin' over this fire and shit. Talkin' bout that's a sign it ain't safe for her and the baby here, but fuck all that. I ain't put that ring on her finger to be in no fuckin' long distance marriage," I continued.

"Don't even stress that shit, T. I got Zo on that shit and by the time she's done, Po's gon' be ringin' yo' phone talkin' 'bout how she's packed and ready to go. You just make sure you ready for that shit 'cuz if you fuck this up, you fuckin' up the peace in my house, nigga. You know how them Orozco sisters are about each other. If yo' bullshit makes Zo come after my head, I'm comin' for yours, nigga."

Zeus was turning onto Cookie's street, but had to slam on the brakes when some kids ran out in front of him just as he cleared the corner.

"Shit! Why the fuck ain't nobody out here watching these kids and shit!" Zeus boomed.

"You know how it is over here, bruh. Hold up for a minute, though. Pull over right here."

There were so many folks up and down the street that it looked like they were having a block party, and with all the shit that had been going on lately, we needed to see who and what was going down before we rode up in the middle of the shit.

Cookie's spot seemed to be jumping with traffic in and out, though it was mostly kids. Zeus and I sat there for a minute or two longer before he shifted back into drive and got ready to ease down the block to Cookie's spot. That was when I looked back down at Cookie's porch and saw some real interesting shit.

"What's up?" Zeus asked when he saw me squinting to make sure I was seeing what I thought I was seeing. I nodded my head down toward the porch, prompting Zeus to follow my gaze and when I heard him grunt, I knew he saw it too.

The nigga that had just exited Cookie's front door looked real familiar, as in our enemy familiar.

"Where we know that nigga from?" Zeus probed, frowning as he was doing his own squint to get a good look at the nigga's face.

"Shrimp... Chateau Margaux... Palme D'or," I offered, seeing how long it would take Zeus to connect the dots.

"Santiago."

Why in the fuck was one of Santiago's men coming out of Cookie's spot like they were homies and shit? I had no idea, but with my wild ass cousin Vinny touching down in a matter of hours, I had no doubt that we would have an answer real soon.

CHAPTER 12

Ares

When I woke up at Zeus' house, I knew that today would be a long one for me. I promised Tori that I would come to her place after I finished with my brothers last night, but I broke that promise on accident. Once we got to choppin' it up about the operation in Cuba and our cousin Vinny coming to town, I guess I lost track of time and nodded off. I already knew that none of that shit would matter to Tori, because I promised that I would come, no matter how late it got. I was sure she stayed up all night waiting for a nigga, too. She blew my phone up from 3:00 to 4:00, so she was gonna be on ten when I did get to her.

Since Titan decided to leave and do his thing, I jumped in my ride and peeled out. I wasn't gon' sit around and wait on this nigga all damn day; I had shit to do, too. There was no doubt that I had to go see Tori, but the plan was to talk to Marisol also. Things had been quiet since the shootout on the freeway, and I needed to see if she had some insight on what was next to come. As soon as I backed out of Zeus' driveway, I picked up the phone to call Tori. I figured she wouldn't answer, so I didn't trip when the voicemail picked up.

As I pulled into Tori's apartment complex, like always, the block was packed. People were scattered about, so I began to scan the crowd, looking for Tori's face. When I didn't see her, I flew into a parking space, then hopped out. The fact that she was not outside hanging with her homies let me further know that she wasn't going to be in a pleasant mood. I could always catch her on the block, prancing around like a stallion, especially with the sun shining like it was today.

I dapped up a few people as I made my way toward Tori's door. I was still looking like yesterday, but I didn't give a damn about that. Besides, no one over here saw me yesterday anyway. I strode up to Tori's door and knocked twice. She didn't answer right away, so I knocked again. I knew that she was home because her car was in the parking lot, and the blinds were wide open in her apartment.

"Tori!" I called out. "Open the door."

"Go away, Ares!"

"T, open the door."

"No, go back to where you been all night."

"Yo, I'm not 'bout to go back and forth with you through this door."

"Well, leave then. I don't feel good, and I don't feel like dealin' with yo' shit or listening to you lie today."

"Just open the door, Tori; we can talk about this face to face."

Tori didn't respond to my suggestion, so I just stood there thinking. What was it about this girl that I couldn't shake? I didn't have to stand outside this door begging to get in, especially when I had plenty of females that would open their doors without a second thought.

"Tori." I knocked again. "If I leave, I promise you that I'm not comin' back."

I was leaning against the door frame, so when she didn't respond, I pushed myself off the door and turned to walk away. Just then, I heard the locks on her door turn. When the door cracked open, I turned back around to face her. Tori was a brown-skinned female, so I grew concerned when she looked pale to me.

"What's wrong with you?" I asked, stepping toward her.

"I don't feel good," she replied, backing away from the door. "I think I ate something bad."

"What you eat?" I questioned, closing the door behind me.

"Where you been?"

Didn't she just say three seconds ago that she didn't feel like this shit today? Here we go.

"At Zeus' house," I answered honestly and directly.

"All night?"

"Yeah, you wanna call him?"

"He's yo' brother; of course, he is gonna have yo' back." She rolled her eyes. "You was probably with a bitch!"

"I'm being honest, but I'm not gon' sit here tryna convince yo' ass! You already know that niggas is gunnin' for me, so I'm out here takin' care of business and, at the same time, tryna keep yo' ass safe. A nigga ain't got time to be with no bitch."

"Whateva."

I strolled over behind her and wrapped my arms around her waist.

103

She tried to pull away from me, but I held her tighter. I wasn't going to let her walk away from me right now. For the first time, I was giving a fuck about her feelings. I didn't want her believing that I was out in these streets fuckin' around when I was really handling business.

"Go get you some clothes and let's ride."

"Where we going?"

"You wanna know what I do all day? Ride with me and see. Then, we'll go to my house."

"I thought yo' house wasn't safe."

"I got another house."

While waiting for Tori to grab some clothes, I chilled on her sofa. For the first time, I saw evidence of what Tori had planned for us last night. Candles were burned all the way down, rose petals were tossed around the room, and there was a half empty bottle of wine sitting on the table. I was already feeling bad about not coming by, but now I was feeling worse. She was really trying to make shit legit between us, but I was unintentionally sabotaging it. Maybe it was time for me to be selfless and take her feelings into consideration.

Tori sauntered back into the living room with three bags hanging from her arms. I knew I'd told her to grab a few things, but it looked like she was low-key moving in. Either way, it really didn't matter because I'd grown to enjoy her company a lil' bit. If I could just get her to stop runnin' her mouth so much, we would get along perfectly.

"Are you all packed?"

"Yeah, can we stop and get something to eat?"

"Sure. What you want?"

"Let's go to The Capital Grille."

"Let's do it."

And just like that, her attitude had gone from kill to chill. The mention of food always changed a female's mood. Hopefully, once she got full, she would be ready to fuck. Shit, I knew I would be.

As soon as we drove out of Tori's apartments, I had to pull over and let her regurgitate. I sat there, looking at her, as she wiped the excess slobber from her mouth. Knowing that I had the look of disgust on my face, I licked my lips and adjusted my look to one of concern.

"You alright?"

"Yeah," she panted.

"What you eat?"

"Everything."

I turned to face forward, but I looked at her out of the side of my eyes. Her ass was probably pregnant and didn't know it, or just hadn't said anything.

"Don't throw up in my car, bro."

I put the car back into drive, then proceeded toward the highway.

"Fuck this car, *bro.*"

"Yeah, whateva."

I mashed the gas on the Porsche Panamera to hurry up and get us to the restaurant. I didn't want to chance her ass throwing up in my shit. My whip was my first lady, and I wasn't gonna let Tori fuck her up.

We made it to the restaurant in record time with no mishaps in the car. Every few minutes, I asked her if everything was alright, but she started to give me attitude after the last time I asked. Knowing that she could flip out on me and show her ass in public at any moment, I kept my mouth closed for the time being. My cell phone rung, redirecting my attention.

"Yo," I picked up, and Tori scowled at me. "You in town?"

"Yeah, man," Vinny beamed through the phone. "Lookin' for that action."

"I already know."

"Where you at? I came over Zeus house, but you not here."

"I'm handlin' some business, I'll be that way in a lil' bit."

"Hurry up, a nigga trigga finger already itchin'."

"A'ight," I laughed.

Vinny was the one person in the family that I related the most to. We both were on some murder gang shit, but we didn't always get to commit any together. What we used to do was compare our body counts, and the tactics we would use. It got so bad that we would torture niggas just to see who could stomach the most blood and guts that poured out of a body. That was my nigga, so I couldn't wait to link up with his ass and bring Santiago down to his knees.

"Where we goin'?" Tori asked as soon as I hung up.

"I gotta go meet up with my kinfolk, so I'mma take you to my house while we handle some business."

"You know, you throw that *handle some business* shit around

106

quite often. You just told whoever you were on the phone with that you were handling business. Is that what I am to you, Ares, business?"

"Nah, you know that."

"No, I really don't. You fuck me whenever you want to, and I still haven't met any of your family."

"Is that what this is about? You want to meet my family?"

"Look Ares, we've been fuckin' around for a minute, and it's time to figure out what it is we are doing? Being a side chick or a hidden chick is not what I am about. It's time for you to come correct, or find someone else to toy with."

"That's what you think? I'm playin' with you? Listen ma, if I wanted to hide you, we wouldn't be out now. A nigga let you spend a night at his place, and I'm takin' you to a house that I don't take anyone to. You get the treatment that nan other bitch ever got from me. A nigga not perfect, but you got to at least applaud my effort."

"I give credit when it's due, but I'm not gon' applaud a bird for flyin'. I know you be on yo' tough guy shit, and it's cute at times, but what do you want? Are you ready to be in a serious relationship or not, because I am."

"Look, I'm takin' the necessary steps to move forward with you, but I do shit my way. Ion need you tryin' to bully me into doing what you want me to do, and how you want me to do it. Just sit back, chill, and take note of a nigga tryin'."

"Who is Marisol?"

And on that note, I just shut down. I knew there was a reason that she had been snappy, but I thought it was because she was sick, but now it all made sense. Ain't no telling how long she'd been waiting to regurgitate Marisol's name to me. What I wasn't gon' do was talk about another female with her. What I did do was wave the waiter down for the check.

"Oh, so you just ain't gon' say shit," Tori continued when we walked out of the restaurant. "One mention of that bitch name got you on mute; she must really be something to you. You fuckin' her too?"

"She ain't shit to me, aight! Get yo' ignant ass in the car, man!"

She snatched the car door open, then slammed it in my face. I casually walked around to the other side and slid in.

"You think I'm a damn fool, Ares! I'm not 'bout to play these games with you. If you want to fuck other bitches, do that, but eliminate me out of the equation."

"You've been talkin' shit for an hour, and I'm gettin' sick of it—"

"Well, we have something in common 'cause I'm sick of yo' shit too," she slammed her fist on the dashboard.

"Bro, don't disrespect my shit."

"Fuck this car!" she punched the dashboard. "You care about this piece of shit more than you care about my feelings?"

I wanted to bump her muthafuckin' head against that dashboard so hard for hitting my shit after I don' already told her Easter basket head ass to stop.

"Keep on, and I'm gon' end up packin' a funeral for yo' ass. Stop actin' like you don't know who the fuck I am!"

"Kill me then, bitch! I don't give a fuck!" She drew her leg back, then kicked the damn dashboard. She had on heels, so it pierced the dash, causing the airbag to fly out and sock her bitch ass in the mouth. Inside, I said, *"that's what the fuck she gets for kicking my shit."* My main bitch kick back was like a Desert Eagle on that ass.

"Baby, you alright?"

"No," she cried.

I hopped out the car and jogged around to her side. She was sitting there bawling when I opened the door. Just a minute ago, she was on some Biggie, *Ready to Die* shit; now, she was all Wonder Bread soft. I pushed the airbag back into the dashboard, then picked up her out of the car.

"If you want this shit to work between us, then you need to stop fightin' with me. Damn, a nigga tryin', but you always on that drama shit."

"I wouldn't be on it if bitches wasn't poppin' up at yo' house while I'm there."

"Who popped up, Marisol?"

"Yeah."

"What did she say?"

"She ain't say shit; she was lookin' for you."

"Why you just now tellin' me this?"

"Because you haven't spent more than five minutes with me since it happened. You fell asleep on me the other night, and last night I didn't even see yo' ass." She looked me in my eyes. "I'm pregnant, Ares."

Goosebumps filled my arms when those words slipped from her lips. I'd been waiting on her to say those words to me, but it was all real now. To be honest, this is the first thing that I had heard today that made me smile.

"I know."

"You know? How you know?"

"'Cause I did it on purpose."

"Why would you do that?"

"Because I want to be with you, and I want a family with you. But, don't have a nigga regrettin' this shit." I kissed her on the lips, then smiled.

"Ugh," she grunted. "I hate that I love yo' yellow ass."

"I feel the same way."

CHAPTER 13

Zeus

"Loni Calhoun, please," I spoke into my phone as I kept an eye on Cookie's crib.

"One moment," the receptionist said as she placed me on hold.

"Why are you bringing Loni into this?" Titan asked, staring a hole in the side of my head.

"If Cookie is fraternizing with the enemy, then I won't be feeding her anymore. Let them niggas do it."

"I think we should just talk to her first," Titan tried to reason with me.

"You go talk to her. My patience has worn thin, and I'm liable to just come down on her."

"Nah, man. You can't just do that. She got kids."

"And? We've been taking care of her and *her kids.* You go give her the opportunity to step away from whatever it is that she is doing, and I will spare her life. She just needs to get the fuck out of Miami before I change my mind."

"Let's go talk to her," Titan said as we both watched the sleek Mercedes that Santiago's flunky drove speed down the street.

"*You* can go talk to her, but I'm staying here," I said with the phone still pressed to my ear.

"This is Loni."

I had to control the blood flow to my lower region as Loni's sultry voice produced music to my ears. Loni Calhoun was just a sexy as her name. She was the color of milk chocolate with perfect, full lips and deep, brown eyes that a nigga could get lost in. She reminded a nigga of Meagan Good. She was petite like my wife with the curves to match. If I could have them both, I would, but Zo was not going for that shit.

"Loni, how are you doing today, beautiful?" I asked with a smirk on my face.

"Zeus DiBiasi? To what do I owe the pleasure?"

"There is an account your bank holds that I opened for Cynthia Carson. I need to freeze it."

"Uh oh, who has pissed you off?" Loni asked. I could hear the smirk in her voice as she typed away on her end. "It's done. Is there *anything* else I can help you with today?"

Heel, boy, I thought to my dick, as it jumped at the thought of Loni's lips wrapped around it. I pushed the thought to the back of my mind as I politely declined her offer and ended the call.

"Let's go," I said, adjusting myself and opening the door.

"Oh, now you want to go? I thought you were too busy phone fucking Loni," Titan chuckled.

"Man, bring yo' ass."

I didn't wait for Titan to get out of the car as I took long strides toward Cookie's front door. I wanted to get to the bottom of her apparent betrayal. I hoped that maybe Cookie did not know the connection that the man had with Santiago and was just dating him. There was nothing wrong with her finding love, as long as it did not interfere with her work with us. I had long moved her from working in the trap houses, and she was now keeping up with the cleaning and the upkeep of various rental properties. After the fire at Titan's place, I could not afford for her to leak that information to anyone associated with Santiago so that they could burn those to the ground as well.

I knocked on the door like I was Miami Dade PD with a warrant. It took less than thirty seconds for Cookie to open the door with a look of alarm on her face. It softened the moment she realized it was me. Her eyes travelled from my face to Titan, who had caught up to me and was now standing behind me. I maintained an even expression on my face. I did not need for her to feel uncomfortable. There was no need for her to suspect anything was wrong, even though I had a suspicion that everything was wrong.

"Zeus? Titan? What are y'all doing here?" she asked, still holding the door.

That was my first clue that something was off with Cookie. She always invited us in when we came over. Now, she was standing at the door as if she was scared for us to come in. I scanned the yard quickly and noticed that the toys that usually cluttered the yard were no longer there. I focused on the children that were playing in the street and noticed that Cookie's girls were not in the fray.

"Just coming to check on you. How are things going?" I said as I focused my attention back on her.

"I can't complain," Cookie answered as her eyes darted up and down the street.

"You're not going to invite us in?" Titan asked. I could tell by his tone that he had also caught on to her strange behavior.

"Oh ... um ... sure. Come in, fellas."

Cookie stood to the side and allowed us to come into the house. The sickly-sweet smell of crack laced with weed immediately attacked my nostrils. I frowned a bit as Cookie shuffled around the house in a vain attempt to straighten up the cluttered living room. To say I was shocked that Cookie's normally clean home was sort of a pig sty would have been an understatement. Cookie never kept a messy house, so I was convinced that she had to be on that shit. I knew just who was supplying her.

"Where are the girls?" I asked as I continued to watch Cookie's hopeless attempt to clean.

"They are with some family up north," Cookie said without looking at me.

"I thought you didn't have any family?" Titan finally spoke up.

"I don't. Their dad's family sent for them. They heard about my accident and thought it was best that they come spend time with them for a while. They didn't approve of my lifestyle ... you know?"

I nodded my head and wondered where all of this so-called

family was when Cookie was living on the streets. I glanced at Titan, who was already typing away on his cell phone. I knew that he was texting Knowledge to get some info. I focused my attention back on Cookie and watched as she continued to move around nervously. It was like she couldn't sit still. As much as I hated to admit it, Cookie had become a liability that needed to be dealt with. I wouldn't make a move, however, until I knew for sure that her girls were in good hands.

"Well Cookie, we won't stay in your hair too long. We were just stopping by to check on you," I said, motioning for Titan to head to the door.

"Oh ... well, thanks for coming by," Cookie mumbled, offering me a weak smile. Her teeth were yellow like she had not brushed them in days or weeks.

Titan gave her a quick head nod as we both exited the house. The fresh air was a welcome commodity as I took a deep breath and headed for the car. We both walked in silence as we crossed the residential street. The sun was starting to set, and a few of the kids had already disappeared back into their homes. I opened the driver's door of my Porsche Panamera and slid into the Italian leather seat.

"What you want to do?" Titan asked as he continued to type away on his phone.

"Find out where her girls are. I'm not making a move until I know they are safe."

"Already on it."

"Cool."

I left Titan to his information gathering. My cell phone chimed, and it was Vin. He had landed in Miami. A smirk danced on my face as I pulled out of the neighborhood. I said a silent Hail Mary and kissed my rosary beads for Cookie. I was definitely going to have to go to confession and speak with Father Rossi at some point in the week.

Ж

"Kill her," Zo said with finality after I told her the information that Knowledge brought back to us. I had to pull my phone away from my ear to make sure that I was still talking to my wife. I knew Zo and her sisters had a crazy side, but I just knew she would talk me out of ending another mother's life and basically leaving her children as orphans.

Knowledge kicked back some information that Cookie's daughters were, in fact, staying with her old man's family in Chicago. He also discovered that her man, Cicero, used to work for Santiago. The bid he was serving was because of Santiago. He was moving weight for him and got hemmed up with the drugs. Cicero refused to name his supplier and was sentenced to twenty-five years for drug trafficking. In the Mexican cartel, losing the drugs was punishable by death. In return, for his silence, Santiago let Cicero and his family live. He also did not provide support to Cookie and the girls afterward. Word got back to Santiago that Cookie was now working for me, and he used one of his men to slip in like the snakes that they were to see if they could get any inside information.

"What about her girls?" I asked, playing toward Zo's maternal side.

"What about them? It sounds to me like they are in good hands,

Zeus. Let them stay where they are. If she wants to be a base head, those girls are better off without her. If she wants to betray us after we got her glass-dick-sucking ass off the streets, she deserves death."

I was surprised that I was the one showing more compassion than my wife was at the moment. Usually, I was the one swinging my iron fist and handing out death sentences for disloyal employees, but I still felt a bit of responsibility for Cookie being injured in the first place. I was the one who got her the job in the trap house. I was also not so big on offing women and children. I wanted to give Cookie the opportunity to get the hell out of Miami, but Ares and Zo were dead set on just eradicating the problem altogether. Whether Cookie knew it or not, she was going to be a casualty of war.

"Zeus? Are you there?" Zo asked.

"I'm here," I replied as I cleared my throat.

"You know what you have to do, right?"

"I know, but it doesn't mean I am going to like it."

"It doesn't matter. You have to do what's right for your empire and your family."

"I know."

"Go say a few Hail Marys. And Zeus?"

"Yeah, babe?"

"Do something about Marisol. She's making Ares weak. I heard about that stunt he pulled. And what's this I hear about him settling down with that chick, Tori?"

"How do you even know all of this?"

117

"You forget, papi. I'm a woman. I don't just live behind the iron gates of our mansion. I keep my ear to the street as well," Zo said with a chuckle.

"I see. Marisol is not making Ares weak, though. If anything, she lit a fire under his ass."

"If you say so, but from what I heard about Tori, she might be a good fit for him. Still, something needs to be done about Marisol. She is a liability. Her connection to Ares is no good for us. It needs to be ended."

"You just killing everybody off, ain't you?" I asked in humor. Zo was continuously proving to me that she was not to be fucked with.

"I'm just clipping loose ends. I love being home in Cuba, but I'm ready to come home."

"I know, babe. I'm ready for you to come home, too."

"I still have four more weeks before you can *cum* anywhere."

I smirked. My wife knew me like that back of her hand. We talked for a few more minutes before she put the girls on the phone. When Apollo started crying, we said our goodbyes. I missed my wife and kids, and Zo was right. I needed to clip these loose ends and cut the snake off at the head. The sooner I did that, the sooner I could have them back in Miami. I knew just the way to get that started, and we needed Marisol for that. She was going to be our bait to draw Santiago out. I was not sure how Ares was going to react to our plan, but like Cookie, Marisol would also be a casualty of our war.

CHAPTER 14

Titan

"Trust me, nigga, pregnant women have no concept of the word no, especially with the first one. Your best bet is to nod and smile at whatever the fuck she wants to buy."

"Bruh, I get that she's excited. Shit, I'm excited too, but damn—seven thousand dollars for a damn tub that the baby is only gon' be able to use for a few months? The fuck?"

Po was my heart, I swear she was, but the further along she got in her pregnancy, the more she was developing a full-blown shopping addiction. Po liked nice things, but she was usually such a low-key and laid back chick, a jeans and sneakers kinda chick—at least as far as I knew. Don't get me wrong; when it was time to turn up and get out in the streets, Po cleaned up nice and would have you thinking she was an A-list celebrity with the way she could bring a room full of men to their knees, but she wasn't the flashy/big spender type. I don't know if it was the pregnancy that was changing that shit or if she was just in a race to see how long it would take her to burn a hole in my American Express Centurion. Every day, Po seemed to hit me with an even more ridiculous thing that the baby *just had to have*. Today, it was a baby bathtub that was blinged out with close to fifty thousand Swarovski-crystals, some exclusive shit that had to be custom made.

"If I don't know shit else, I know about pregnant women, so believe me when I say it's best to let her have her way for now and make that shit up on the back end. You even fix your mouth to tell her no and she's gon' get in her feelings; then, she's gon' get mad; then, she's gon' get vengeful and start playin' dirty with your ass. You already got a six-week drought to look forward to after she gives birth, and that's assuming there's no complications with anything, so don't do shit to fuck up the pussy supply. Trust me, bruh. Stay on her good side and make sure you get all the ass you can get before she pops because that six weeks is gon' feel like a lifetime." Zeus chuckled, and I supposed he was right. He'd been through this pregnancy stuff three times with Zo. Then again, Zo wasn't exactly the kind of chick you could really tell no anyway.

"I swear I don't wanna be like y'all niggas when I grow up. Up in here sounding like two old ass men and shit. Keep fuckin' round and your women will have your balls on a chain around their necks and be the ones telling yo' ass no!"

Ares couldn't enter a room quietly if his life depended on it. I heard his feet the minute he hit the foyer, but I figured he would head off in search of Vinny before he got up with us.

"Says the nigga that stays with a flock of bitches cussin' him out." I smirked.

"But I bet they ass know what the word *no* means, nigga. Where the fuck my ace at?"

I was surprised it took Ares this long to get here after Vinny called him, but as much shit as he talked, I bet his ass rushed right over to Tori's spot to fuck his way back into her good graces. I meant to clown that nigga on how it looked like Tori had that ass in check like a well-trained puppy, but we had more pressing shit to tend to, so I'd get at him about being whipped later.

"The question is, where the fuck you been? What's good, man?"

Vinny appeared behind Ares in the doorway to Zeus' man cave, and you would have thought Ares was a kid that had been let loose at Disney World. His face lit up, and him and Vinny got so deep off into their man-hug/dap that it was like me and Zeus weren't even sitting there.

"If y'all are done with that long-lost bromance shit, we can get down to business because we got an unexpected detour to make," Zeus cut in, drawing all of our attention to the table of refreshments he'd set up—refreshments as in cognac and cigars.

"Me and Titan ran up on some very disturbing shit today, and after consulting my advisor, it's lookin' like this bitch Cookie gotta go," Zeus announced, catching me so off-guard that I choked on the smooth, amber liquor that I'd just tossed back. Ain't no way in hell Zo told his ass to dead Cookie.

"Yo, you serious about this shit?" I spoke once I reached the tail end of my fit of coughing that kicked off when the liquor went down the wrong way.

"As a heart attack," Zeus confirmed.

"Hold up. What the fuck happened? She got kids and shit," Ares interjected.

"And per my advisor, they'll be better off without her, so it's a done deal. Ares, since you and Vinny are so eager to light some shit up, y'all can handle it—and don't blow no shit up. Keep it low-key like some thieves in the night type shit," Zeus instructed before rattling off some other information that he had pulled together to share with all of us.

My phone started jumping in my pocket with a call from Knowledge, so I stepped out into the hall to take the call because I knew he was calling with some info that I needed to make a move on before the end of the day. Knowledge was definitely one of those *ace in the hole* type niggas, and hearing the information he had to deliver, I made a note to hit him off nicely with a hefty bonus because that nigga truly went above and beyond for the DiBiasis.

When I re-entered the room, Zeus was about halfway through getting Vinny up to speed on the ins and outs of the war we had going on with Santiago. Just hearing him give a rundown of all the attacks Santiago had launched against us brought everything into perspective. We were legit at war with the head of the fucking Mexican cartel. This was the kind of shit that Pops used to tell us about—even warn us about. He always said that more money meant more power, and that was where the problems came in. Most people thought the problems came with the money, but that wasn't the case at all.

See, man was a creature that was competitive by natural instinct. Survival of the fittest was the most common way of describing it, but in a nutshell, life in its most basic form was about survival. You couldn't eat if the next person snatched up the meal before you could get to it, and the prey never made it to the meal if the predator was able to make the prey its meal first. That's what shit came down to. Money made people jealous, but power made people vengeful, and that was what we were dealing with at the end of the day. Santiago was swimming in just as much wealth as we were; it was our power that he had to extinguish to get his point across and further his own agenda, but that nigga was about to be a dead man that was *formerly* powerful since he made the decision to keep fuckin' with me and my family.

"The only question I have is why this muthafucka is still breathing. You guys are DiBiasis, gotdammit, so you should have been taken this fool out and called it a day!" Vinny boomed.

"Man, what you said. That's what the fuck I been tryin' to say all along!" Ares co-signed the sweltering venom that was heating up right there in Zeus' man cave.

I knew Vinny was just what we needed to take care of this shit with Santiago so we could bring our families home, but a part of me wondered what cost that peace would come at. Vinny was a firm believer that if he had to ask for forgiveness in advance for some shit, there would be maximum bloodshed to make it worth his while. Judging by the split second he'd just spent kissing the medallion he sometimes wore in honor of the patron saint he was named after, my gut told me shit was about to get real messy.

"I love you like a brother, cousin, but you ain't gon' like what I'm about to say. I'm on the outside lookin' in, and from what I see, this

Marisol chick is a serious impediment that needs to be handled," Vinny spoke, locking his gaze on Ares to send a clear message that he stood firm in his assessment. My head swung over to Zeus to see if he was thinking the same thing I was. Meanwhile, Ares was true to his name.

"Man, this is bullshit! Fuck!" Ares sprung to his feet and flipped the table over with minimal effort, sending our glasses, cigars, ashtrays, and the decorative table accents flying across the room. One of the items smacked Vinny upside the head on its journey toward the wall.

"Yo, calm the fuck down! You know that shit is true, cuz, so stop letting pussy cloud your fuckin' judgment!" Vinny barked as he walked up on Ares.

There wasn't much height difference between the two, so they were essentially standing eye to eye, but with the collective amount of ignorance that now stood before Zeus and me, I chuckled at how interesting this whole counterattack against Santiago was about to be. We brought Vinny into town to help us dead shit with Santiago, but we had to make sure we kept them niggas' fury aimed in the right direction.

"Both of y'all muthafuckas need to chill, or I'mma be the one catching a body up in here. Ares, break some more shit up in here and I'mma break my foot off in your ass."

"Fuck this shit!" Ares snapped before turning to leave the room, heading off to who knows where. Hopefully, the nigga would go grab a popsicle or something to cool his ass off. I understood his anger, especially in light of losing the seed he previously had on the way with Marisol, but Vinny was right. At the end of the day, Marisol was still the enemy's daughter, so it wasn't even realistic to expect her loyalty to lie with us, no matter how good Ares dicked her down.

I stood to help clean up the mess that Ares' wild ass had just made, but paused when I saw Zeus looking down at his phone with a deep scowl on his face.

"You straight, bruh?" I asked.

"I don't know, but we 'bout to find out," he answered as he got to his feet and explained how he just got a notification that the sensor had been triggered at his front gate, signaling that an unknown vehicle had just entered his property.

Knowledge had hooked Zeus up with a top-of-the-line intrusion detection system to keep a detailed account of everyone that breached his property line. Everyone with clearance to enter his home had a special transponder affixed to their vehicle, and the transponder had to be scanned and approved before the gate would open. There was also a ground sensor that detected vehicle movement, so if a vehicle was detected without the accompanying scan of a transponder, the system would throw a silent alarm notification that was wirelessly delivered to pre-selected devices, including both Zeus and Zo's mobile phones.

Zeus crossed the floor of his man cave, which was now littered with the remnants of Ares' tantrum, and snatched up the remote to bring the sixty-five-inch TV to life that was mounted on one of the walls. Changing the input selection, he brought up a split screen view of the live security feed for his home, and after checking the view afforded by the various cameras, our eyes were drawn to two of the feeds that covered a portion of the front of his home. We looked on as an all-black SUV crept up the driveway toward the house.

"Shit!"

We all sprang into action, and though Zeus had an eerie calmness about him, his eyes told just how fucked up he felt and just what his thoughts were in that moment. If he couldn't keep the place he laid his head safe and protected from outside threats, how the fuck could he bring his family back here in good conscience? He didn't have to say it, but I knew that we were both thinking the same thing: Santiago.

Vinny and I were racing down the main hall now and headed toward the front door. Zeus was bringing up the rear as he used the remote override feature on his phone to secure all the other points of access to his home—more of the **007 James Bond** shit Knowledge was good for.

"The fuck is y'all niggas—"

Ares was exiting a powder room just off the main hall, and we damn near ran him over with our stampede. Seeing the heat that was gripped in each of our hands, he cut his question short and assumed the position, pulling his own piece from his waistband and falling right in line with the three of us. We were just a few feet from Zeus' front door, but I had to choke back a throat full of laughter as I took a quick, sweeping gaze to make sure everyone was in a good position to handle whatever the fuck was on the other side of that door. This dude Vinny had a whole fuckin' AR-15 locked and ready to go, and the custom clip let me know that it wasn't from Zeus' stash. A true DiBiasi, that's what he was.

Zeus gave us all a signal to kill the noise just as we heard a knock ring out on the other side of the door. He slid his phone out, I assumed to check the surveillance feed since there was a camera that was mounted to capture an unobstructed view of the front door. I was positioned just a few feet behind Zeus, off to his left, so I was able to catch a small glimpse of the image on his phone screen. He tossed a look over his shoulder, then brought the phone up into plain view to reveal the source of the knock: a young girl dressed in a brown vest with a hundred-watt smile.

Four grown ass men, creeping through a big ass house on some sneak attack shit, a mini-arsenal of high-powered weapons, ready to blow a hole through the front of Xiamora's dream house—all behind a harmless girl scout.

"Shit," Zeus chuckled, sliding his Glock 17 back on safety before setting it on the shelf in a small alcove that flanked the front door. He gave us all a nod to stand down as he unlocked the door and eased it open to greet the little girl.

"Hi, Mr. DiBiasi. Is Ms. Mora home?"

The little girl sounded like she was ready and eager to launch into her sales pitch.

"I'm sorry, sweetie, but she's not here right now. Did you need to leave something for her?"

One of the main things that let me know my brother was destined to be a father was how he went from a pillar of muscle to a mass of mush when it came to kids, especially little girls. With the way his eyes lit up just talking to the little girl, a person would never guess that not even sixty seconds prior, Zeus was ready to commit as many acts of murder as his clip would allow.

"Aww, man. She said I could see Baby 'Pollo," the little girl sighed, dropping her head with disappointment.

"Tell you what. I'll let her know you stopped by and tell her that you need your very own visit with Baby Apollo the minute she gets back. Will that work?"

The little girl's head shot up and once again, she was flashing a smile that had probably finessed Zeus' subdivision out of a small fortune for her baked goods.

"Ms. Mora always buys the Samoas from me, but I only have four boxes left, and I don't want to make her sad if I run out," the little girl continued.

"How 'bout this: I'll take those four boxes off your hands and surprise Ms. Mora with them when she comes home. Do you think she'll like that?" Zeus bargained.

Nodding her head vigorously, the little girl turned to wave at the vehicle that was idling in Zeus' driveway. She took off running toward the vehicle, slipped beyond the back passenger door, and then resurfaced with two arms full of cookies that I hoped would last until Zo got home. There were three things Xiamora DiBiasi didn't play about: her man, her kids, and her annual supply of Girl Scout Cookies.

"You owe me sixteen dollars, Mr. DiBiasi," little sunshine smiled, holding her hand out for her payment once Zeus had relieved her of the cookies.

"Here's twenty, and you can keep the change, sweetheart." Zeus winked, making the little girl's day. She was so happy that she took off running toward the vehicle and hopped in. We saw the front passenger window ease down as the little girl and the driver waved their departure, then rounded the driveway to exit Zeus' property.

"Bruh, you had us 'bout to blast lil' cookie connect? Yoooooo!"

Vinny and Ares fell out laughing, and I had to get in on the chuckle because damn, shit almost got real. Even Zeus cracked a smile at how we were locked and loaded over the little girl from down the street.

"All bullshit aside, though, that just goes to show you how shit done gone too far with this Santiago dude. Got y'all so on edge you'll fuck around and take out a whole wall over a damn house fly."

"Let's map this shit out then so we can handle shit and get you back home before you and Ares take the whole city out. Wild ass animals," Zeus mumbled as he left us standing in the foyer and headed back toward his man cave.

"Ay, lemme hold summa them cookies right quick," Ares spoke.

"Sure, if you wanna end up holdin' your eye once Zo finds out you ate her shit."

Ж

"Still no word from her?" Knowledge probed.

"Negative, so I got some moves we need to make on that."

I met up with Knowledge to look at some blueprints he had for some demolition and renovations that I wanted to do with the setup of our current operations. That shit we saw down in Cuba still had my brain jumpin', and with Knowledge just as geeked up as me, I was trying to get something up and running ASAP so we could work out the kinks and get all our shit streamlined.

"Well, I was gonna wait until we finished this business today to show this to you, but I think you gon' wanna see this now," Knowledge spoke as he reached over into what I called his bag of tricks. He withdrew a tablet, swiped through a bunch of files, cued up a video, and passed it in my direction.

Right there before my eyes was a perfectly okay India, pulling into her driveway, sliding out of her car, and bouncing off toward her front door. It looked like she may have been fresh from the gym considering her attire and the fact that her normally bone-straight hair was pulled up on top of her head in a frizzy ponytail.

"The fuck?" I frowned.

"My guy's been sitting on her for the past two days. Seen her coming and going pretty carefree. Even stepped out in her Sunday's best last night. Looks alive and well to me, boss man."

That she did, which really had me wondering why the fuck she hadn't got at me and even seemed to be dodging me. I'd left her no less than a dozen messages, but slacked off once I knew she wasn't the one killed when my shit burned down. The last message I sent asked her to just shoot me a quick reply to let me know she was okay, and that I'd leave her alone after that because I knew she was probably mad at a nigga. I knew I should have ended things the right way with her before I headed out to Cuba, but shit, I just ran short on time and figured I could deal with it when I got back. Now, I was feeling like I had really fucked up because she was moving funny as hell, and I didn't know exactly why.

"One more thing, boss man." Knowledge reached out for the tablet, and I passed it to him as he went to work again. A few swipes later, he passed it back over to me.

"It was a little more difficult than I expected, but I was able to enhance the video from your spot and pull some still images."

"Yooo, what the fuck?"

I was frowning at the tablet yet again as I swiped through one image after another that gave a clear view of the person that was caught in various stages of motion, dressed in all black as they approached the maid's quarters at the rear of what used to be my house. The camera had even caught a quick shot of the person smiling at one point.

The person was none other than India.

"I went ahead and installed a few cameras around her spot, even set up a few mics so we can hear what's going down on the inside to find out what she knows and who she's talking to," Knowledge offered. I gave him a nod of approval as he proceeded to pack up the rest of the items we had spread out across the table.

Damn, this was my nigga! I swore they didn't make 'em no more thorough than him. It was looking like India burned my house down, and I just couldn't wrap my mind around the shit. I knew she was feeling some type of way once she found out that Po was pregnant, but for her to burn my shit down meant she was on some *get back by any means necessary* shit. That put a whole new spin on things since she'd now become one of those loose ends Zeus was saying that we needed to handle before we could breathe easy enough to bring our families back. I now understood why Ares stormed off earlier at the mention of Marisol because although I didn't necessarily love India, a small piece of me cared for her and didn't wish any ill will toward her, but shit. I had to protect my wife-to-be and my unborn at any cost, and if that meant India had to pay with her life, then so be it.

CHAPTER 15

Ares

*O*nce Vinny mentioned killing Marisol, my emotions took over my mind. Although I didn't have strong feelings for Marisol, I still couldn't stomach the thought of killing her. I couldn't stomach the thought of killing her or Cookie, because women were never on my radar. True enough, both women did pose a threat to our empire, but I didn't want either of their blood on my hands. As much as I loved to squeeze the trigger on my M1911, I think I might have to fall back and let Vinny handle it on his own.

"So, what's up, Ares," Vinny spoke, taking a drag from the blunt. "We doing this tonight or what?"

We were chilling in the back of the strip club, waiting for Black and Poody to show up. Shit with the business was going to shift, so I had to get them up to date on what's to come. Plus, they needed to update me on how business was going. Santiago was on a nigga's mind so heavy that I had to put them in charge of checking on the traps for me.

"Are you sure that we have to kill them?"

"Cookie is a liability to your organization. She knows too much, she's conversing with your enemy, and she's on that pipe, so we don't have a choice."

"But, what about Marisol?"

"Cuz, look, I know she was yo' first baby mama or whatever, but y'all been chasing this muthafucka Santiago for too long. If we want to see that man, we gotta give him a reason to show his face."

Though I didn't want to admit it out loud, Vinny was right about everything. Marisol was the apple of Santiago's eye, so he would come out of his hiding hole, no doubt, if we had his prized possession on the chopping block. I just can't be the one to do it; a nigga will never be able to sleep a wink if I watched the life disappear from her eyes.

"A'ight, this is what's gon' happen. I'mma ride with you to take care of Cookie, but that Marisol situation, you gon' have to handle that with someone else. I'll get her where you need her to be, but I'm not helpin."

"You gettin' soft on me, but I understand. I'll take care of that myself."

"Cool."

I looked up and saw Poody walking toward us, dapping up a few niggas along the way. Black was right behind him doing the same shit.

When Poody and Black approached the table, I introduced them to Vinny. As soon as they took their seats, I jumped right into it, telling them about what was to come. I went ahead and let them know about Cookie and Marisol also. Neither one of them seemed to give a fuck about it, so that conversation was a quick one. They brought me up to date on how everything was going at the houses. Like always, shit was running smooth like water.

"So, once we get this shit taken care of, we'll start this new operation."

"When we gon' get this nigga, Santiago?" Black questioned.

"Like I said, once Vinny gets Marisol, he'll come out to play. Make sure yo' crews stay on alert, 'cause ain't no tellin' what he might pull out of his bag of tricks."

"I got something for that ass, though," Vinny smiled. "I'm ready to get this shit poppin'."

"We got a few more hours, just chill and watch this ass floatin' around here."

"You right, I need her right there," he said, pointing at Naomi.

I hadn't seen Naomi in a good lil' minute, so I kind of lit up inside at the sight of her. She was eyeballing me and smiling, so I nodded her over. Vinny wanted a dance from her, but I'd be the one taking it. Besides, she already knew that she couldn't dance for anyone in my crew—at least when I'm around, she can't.

Naomi walked right up on me and pulled me up from my seat. We shared a hug, and I couldn't help but to grab a handful of that ass. I mean, it was just sitting there. When I removed my hands from around her, Vinny had his eyes planted on us. He gave me that *fuck you*, nigga look, but he didn't speak on it. He already knew the deal, so he waved down the first chick that he saw to get a lap dance. Naomi grabbed my hand, then led me toward the champagne room.

Once we entered, I took a seat in the middle of the loveseat, and Naomi took her seat on my lap. She was still rocking that smile on her face when she turned to look at me. I can tell by the look in her eyes that she wanted to fuck, and it took me back to the night I hit her off. Her pussy had some fire power, but she didn't have anything on Tori.

"Where you been, Ares? I ain't seen you in a hot lil' minute."

"I've been handlin' business. You know shit has been hectic lately."

"I heard."

"But, you know, shit is being handled."

"You need to relax," she rubbed her hands over my manhood. "You need me to relieve some tension for you?"

I looked at her for more than a few seconds before answering. A nigga could use some head right now, but at the same time, I needed to keep my head on straight. My mind had to be right when I got to Cookie's house so shit could run smoothly.

"Nah, I'm good."

She looked at me all surprised and shit. I ain't gon' lie, I surprised my damn self with that statement. I'd never turned down ass in my life, especially not ass that had fire power. Immediately, I started to think about Tori—at that moment, I knew that she had a hold on me that I would never be able to shake. When I was with a female that was as fine as Naomi, no other female had ever popped up in my head.

"You must got you a lil' girlfriend or something," she quizzed.

"Something like that."

"You're kiddin', right?" I sat there looking at her with my serious face. "Oh my, I need to see the chick that made Ares DiBiasi settle down."

I chuckled, "She mean, you don't wanna meet her."

"I can only imagine; any women that fools with you has to be mean. Especially to keep yo' wild ass in line."

"You're right about that. Gone and give me my dances so I can get up outta here."

She stood up from my lap, then began to slow wind her body. I made myself more comfortable on the loveseat to watch the show. Fuck it, I may as well enjoy this moment, because there was no telling when I would be back.

After a few dances from Naomi, we emerged from the champagne room and headed back over to the table. Tick had shown up, and they were all enjoying themselves. I gave Vinny a look to let him know that it was time to roll. He downed the rest of his liquor, then stood up from the table. We dapped up the guys before heading toward the front door. Black was still watching my back, so he trailed out of the club behind us. He wasn't going to participate in the murder, but he was going to stick back to watch and make sure no one saw us.

I pulled up in front of Cookie's house and parked. It was late, so the street was quiet, unlike normal. Vinny and I sat in the car hitting the last of the blunt we were smoking on. I looked in the rearview mirror, and I could see Black parked half a block back.

"So, this is what's gon' happen," I inhaled. "I'mma go knock on the door, she gon' let me in, and I'm gon' go to the bathroom. I'll let the window up, so you can enter through there. While I'm talkin' to her, you come in and handle up."

"A'ight," he said, slipping on a pair of rubber gloves.

"Wait 'til you hear me say 'a'ight then' before you come in, though. If she sees you, off top she gon' know what's up. I don't want her to scream on our ass."

"I got you."

"Let's go."

We both jumped out of the car. While I walked straight toward the front door, Vinny ran around back of the apartment. Before I knocked, I looked up the block at Black. He flashed his headlights, then I knocked on the door. I could hear music playing down low in the apartment, along with the sounds of someone moving around. Patience had never been my thang, so immediately, I knocked again.

"Who is it," she called out.

"Ares."

The music went off, the locks started twisting, then the door came open. The apartment was dark, only lit with a few candles that were scattered out. I stood there looking at her closely because she was high as a kite right now. Her eyes were barely opened, and she had this blank look on her face.

"What you doing here, Ares," she smiled with them chapped lips while scratching her arm.

"I came to check up on you. What you got going on," I asked, pushing past her into the apartment. "You on a date?"

"Nah," she sniffed. "I forgot to go down there and pay my light bill. But, I'm going in the morning."

"You good, you need some money?"

"Yeah, I need to send something to my kids."

"I gotcha. Let me go use the bathroom real quick."

"You know where it is," she slurred, then plopped down on the sofa.

I walked down the long hallway, stumbling over shit and making my way toward the bathroom. It was evident that she was on something because Cookie never kept a nasty house. She had fallen off bad, and that shit hurt to see. I guess it would be better for us to go ahead and put her out of her misery before shit got worse. I felt sorry for her kids, but they would be better off without her anyway.

I flushed the toilet with my elbow and turned the faucet on with the back of my hand, then pushed the window up with my knuckles. I had to make sure not to leave my fingerprints anywhere in this house. I stuck my head out of it to see if I could see Vinny. As soon as I did, his ass popped up in the window smiling. He damn near scared the shit out of me, but I didn't dare show it. I stepped back so that he could climb in, then I turned the water off. When he pulled a string of rope from his pocket, I couldn't help but to smirk and shake my head at him. How long had his crazy ass been walking around with that damn rope in his pocket?

"Yo," I said as I stepped back into the living room. "What's going on with this house? Don't tell me the rumors I'm hearin' about you being on that shit is true."

"Who said that?" she asked, now rubbing her chest.

"The streets are talkin'. If you are, you can't work for us. But, from what I heard, you're workin' with someone else anyway."

"Who? Who am I workin' with, Ares? First, you come in here accusing me of being on drugs, now I'm workin' with someone else? What is going on?"

"You tell me. That's why I'm here, to find out what the fuck is going on!"

"I swear to God, Ares, ain't nothing going on." She began to scratch again. "I'm not working with Mondo."

She just fucked up. I never even said who she was working with; now, she just spit out the name of one of Santiago's flunkies out of nowhere.

"And, you swear to God?"

"Yes."

"A'ight then, come lock the door behind me."

I traveled over to the door, then waited for her to open it.

"You're not gonna kill me, are you Ares?"

"You know I wouldn't dare lay a hand on you."

"Oka—" she began to say, but Vinny wrapped the rope around her neck.

She was looking at me with her eyes bucked, like she was begging me to help her. I would have almost felt guilty about the shit, but she had fucked up by mentioning Mondo's name. I stood there watching until her body went limp, then Vinny drug her body over to the couch. He laid her down, I walked out of the front door, and Vinny closed it behind us. I didn't have on gloves, so I made sure not to touch shit with my fingers.

After dropping Vinny back off at Zeus' house, I headed straight home to Tori. I was gon' get out and talk to Zeus about what happened, but I didn't want to accidentally spend a night over there and have to fight about it. I was trying to keep shit cool between us so that I didn't stress her out while she's carrying my seed. Since I was in my car that I do dirt in, I drove around to the back of the house, where I had a second garage. It held three different cars that I switched out every time I committed a crime in it. Now, I had to get rid of this car and get another piece of shit to do dirt in.

When I strode into the house, I didn't hear anything. It was late, so I was sure that Tori was in a deep sleep. She was always asleep, but stayed complaining about me not being home. I guess she expected me to stay at home and watch her ass sleep all day. That wasn't even an option for me, but after Santiago was taken care of, I would try to spend more time with her.

I pushed the door to the bedroom open, and Tori was sitting in the middle of the bed with her lingerie on. The room was lit with candles, reminding me of the dark hellhole I just came from.

"Hey, baby," she winked.

"Damn," was all I could say as I walked toward her.

"I missed you today."

"I missed you too," I kissed her.

"Get naked," she commanded.

"Let me take a shower first."

"Why you gotta take a shower first?"

"Because, I got death on me. I'm not 'bout to fuck you with that on me."

She laid back on the bed and looked up at the ceiling. I walked toward the bathroom, removing my clothes in the process.

"And, wash that cheap ass Victoria's Secret body spray off you!"

"Okay," I said, then closed the door behind me.

Fuck, I hope that lap dance didn't cost me my piece of ass tonight. If it did, we would both be pissed 'cause I was arguing her ass down tonight.

I took a quick shower—one of the quickest I'd ever had. I didn't want to give Tori time to ponder to herself and come at me with no fuck shit that would ruin the mood. Not tonight. She was still laid back on the bed when I walked into the bedroom, newborn naked. I strolled over to the side of the bed, then stood there looking at her.

"I guess you mad now?"

"You didn't smell like death to me, but there can definitely be a funeral soon," she spat.

"Kill that noise. We had a lil' meeting at the strip club earlier, and you know how them thirsty hoes be. I couldn't leave without getting a dance. Come here." I pulled her by her ankles toward me. "You done got all sexy for me; now you sitting here mad for nothing."

"I'm not mad."

"Well, gimme this pussy then."

I pushed her legs open, and her clit greeted me with a smile. She had on a pair of thongs with the crotch area cut out, so everything was exposed. Her pussy was already glistening from her juices, but I dove in head first to get that monkey extra wet.

Once I licked her to her first nut, I slowly entered her tunnel. I always had to enter Tori slow because her pussy be snatching. If I moved too fast, a nigga might fuck around and burst too quick. The first time we fucked, I did that shit and if I remember correctly, I burst in like three minutes. It was supposed to be a quickie anyway, but a nigga wasn't tryin' to come before seven minutes, period. Tori wrapped her legs around my waist as I dug into her deeper.

"Why you cheatin," I kissed her. "Open them legs up!"

"Shhiit," she whined. "You too deeeep!"

I slowed my rhythm down, then started long-stroking her. Since I was still standing on the side of the bed, I stepped back a little. I wasn't trying to kill the pussy, so I had to back up off it and stroked her slowly. Listening to her moan made my temperature rise higher than it already was. That shit was hypnotic; next thing you know, I was back in them guts.

"Fuck, Ares!"

"You love me?"

"Yaass!"

"You bet not ever betray me." I slapped her on the bottom of her butt cheek. "You hear me?"

"Yes, Daddy."

143

"If you do, I'll kill you my muthafuckin' self."

Her moans stopped, and she gazed into my eyes. I slowed my strokes to focus on her.

"You're the father of my child. I would never betray you, no matter what."

"Bet not. And if I ever catch you doing any drugs, beside weed, I'll choke yo' ass to death."

"I wouldn't expect anything less."

I slid my arm under the small of her back, then climbed in the bed with her. She wrapped her arms around me and pulled me in for a kiss. We tongue kissed each other hard as I started my slow grind against her. I had never made love before, but tonight, that was exactly what I was going to do. It was obvious that I loved this girl, so it was time for me to start showing it since I couldn't bring myself to say those actual words.

CHAPTER 16

Zeus

I sat in the corner, taking long pulls from the fresh Cuban cigar. Vinny had really come through for a nigga. Now, as I studied her hazelnut-colored skin as it struggled against the nylon ropes, I could see exactly why my brother ran up in Marisol. The bitch was fine. You could almost forget she was Mexicana. Marisol was stacked just like a sista, although I had a suspicion she'd bought some of those curves. I made a note to ask Ares later as I took a sip of my Louis XIII.

"Why do you have me here?" she finally asked, abandoning her feeble attempts at freeing herself.

"Why do you think?" I asked with a smirk. Marisol was a Santiago. I was more than certain that Francisco had put her up on game.

"I don't know. I have nothing to do with my father's business."

"I thought you said that you didn't know."

"You look familiar," she said with her perfectly arched eyebrows nearly touching, as if she were trying to recall a memory.

"I probably do." I shrugged.

Marisol's attention was temporarily taken from me as Bones entered the empty warehouse we used for these sort of things. I could smell the food from Pollo Tropical through the bag that he had in his hand. My stomach instantly started to growl as he set the food that reminded me of Cuba on the table in front of me. I had not realized how hungry I was until I opened the take-out box and got the full whiff of the Trios Chicken Platter. I said my grace quickly, and as I was about to dive in, I stole a quick glance at Marisol. Her mouth was practically watering at the aroma that was quickly filling the room.

"You hungry?" I asked as I tore the top off the takeout box.

"You don't have to do that, Z. I got her something." Bones stopped me from sharing my food and pulled out a third box of food.

I watched as Bones put a small folding table in front of Marisol and untied her hands.

"Don't try to run. I will shoot you before you make it to the door," he warned.

I swallowed a chuckle as I dug into my food. Ares still did not know that we were holding her here. If his reaction was anything close to what he displayed in my office, he was not going to be happy. I figured the best way to deal with my brother and his temper would be head-on. I understood the fact that Marisol was the first woman to ever carry his seed, but she was no longer carrying it, and she was a liability.

I sent Ares a text and told him to meet us at the warehouse. Vinny had not told him that he had picked up Marisol, and that was under my orders. I knew he would feel some sort of betrayal from Vinny and myself, but we were in war, and he knew, out of everyone, that feelings did not matter in war. He was going to have to get on board with ending this shit and needed to realize that Marisol was the key to all of it. Killing off Santiago's camp was not getting us anywhere in this war. We needed to change our approach. I knew that I would lay down my life for my daughters and my son, so I was more than certain that using Marisol as bait would draw him out. So far, he had been harder to locate than Osama Bin Laden, but I was about to Obama the situation.

"Damn, I can't believe Vinny's crazy ass came through," Titan said in disbelief.

"Why would you doubt him? He's just as crazy as Ares. You can't doubt the Italian Stallion. That dude specialized in snatching people up. You heard how he did Cookie," I explained, wiping my mouth.

"Yeah, I heard that," Titan replied, placing his bag on the table.

Knowledge entered behind him and did the same. They started pulling out laptops and other tech devices that I knew nothing about, so I sat back down and finished my food. Bones, however, was in awe and started picking up some of the components, only to have them taken out of his hand by Knowledge. I chuckled a bit as my eyes swept over to Marisol, who had stopped eating. Her eyes were glued to us, and a look of shock and betrayal had planted itself on her face.

"That's why I know you," Marisol spoke quietly. "You know he won't stand for this. Family or not, Ares wouldn't let anything happen to me."

Titan chuckled a bit. Marisol clearly did not know Ares as well as she thought. I knew that my baby brother was not big on killing women and children, and I did not want to kill Marisol if we didn't have to, but

I knew she would be a loose end. I did not do loose ends. If we let her live, she could try to seek revenge on us for killing her father. We would always have to watch our backs, especially with the resources that she could get her hands on. I would not be comfortable with bringing my family home as long as I knew there was someone out there that was at our heads. If we killed her, that would end Santiago's bloodline since she was an only child and the majority of our problems.

Sure, the Mexicans would only name a new head, but most smart bosses operated with as little conflict as possible. They did not want unneeded attention. This is how we moved. More importantly, this is also how we remained outside of prison walls. Francisco Santiago did not understand those rules. He moved recklessly, and we...well, Ares reacted in the way he saw fit. Unfortunately, Ares' reaction is what started this whole downhill spiral, but I could see that we were very close to it ending it.

"You don't know my brother very well," I stated as I moved to tie her back up.

"You're wrong. He would never let anything happen to me. He's killed for me."

"You're wrong. He didn't kill for you; he killed for your unborn baby. Tell me something, Marisol, did your father really make you have an abortion? I've been thinking a lot about that, and I could not imagine any good Catholic choosing abortion, no matter how much you loathed the father."

I saw Marisol's face falter. She recovered quickly, but not quick enough for me to miss it. *I knew it*, I thought to myself. Something deep down inside of me told me that Santiago would never consider abortion. As evil or as much of a criminal as he was, he was still what we all were—Catholic.

The Catholic Church teaches that human life is created and begins at the moment of conception. They see abortion as the termination of an unborn life, and therefore, it's always wrong, sinful, and immoral. The circumstances by which that life was conceived are considered irrelevant. I would never use this newly found information to sway my brother into doing something that he was not comfortable with, but I did feel like he deserved to know the truth before Marisol left this earth.

"You're going to tell him," I demanded.

"Please, you don't understand. I—" Marisol started.

"What doesn't he understand?" Ares' voice reverberated through the nearly empty warehouse. A look of fear replaced the pleading eyes that Marisol once wore.

I turned around to see my brother and Vinny standing in the warehouse's garage-style door dressed in all black. Ares' caramel-colored skin started to take a red hue as I could see the anger rising in him.

"Man, why the fuck y'all got her tied up like that?" Ares said as he marched over to Marisol and began to undo her ropes. The relief that had momentarily come over her was short-lived when he spoke again. "What won't he understand, Marisol?"

"I-I can't say," she whispered with her head down in shame.

"You better get to saying something," Ares demanded, removing his pistol from his back holster. Marisol shifted her weight nervously from one foot to the other.

"My father did not make me get an abortion." Her voice was barely above a whisper as she kept her eyes glued to the floor.

"What do you mean? Is yo' ass still pregnant?" Ares asked. His agitation was growing in his voice.

Marisol did not open her mouth. Ares stood there, seething. I could see his mind running a mile a minute. I wanted to step in and diffuse the situation, but my brother deserved to know the truth.

"Man, Marisol, you better say something before I leave yo' wetback ass stankin'!" Ares barked.

I could tell by the look on Marisol's face that she had never heard Ares' rude ass speak to her that way. I was pretty sure that no one had ever spoken to her ass like that. She was what I called a mafia princess. They sat pretty, did not get their hands dirty, and reaped all the rewards that their parents put in. I hated bitches like that. My daughters would never rely on others to do all the dirty work. Athena and Perry would be bosses in their own right.

"No, I'm not pregnant," Marisol finally spoke up. She rested her eyes on Ares.

I could see the hurt in my brother's eyes as he raised the gun and rested it in between Marisol's eyes. Even though our end objective was to end Marisol, I couldn't let him do it just yet. I stepped forward and rested my hand on the barrel of his weapon.

"You can't right now, bruh," I said sympathetically. "You will get your chance, but it can't be now."

Ares seemed to come out of a trance as he turned to look at me. I could see tears start to cloud his eyes as his grip on his gun loosened. Marisol had hurt him to the core. He released the gun and slowly turned to walk away. If my reflexes weren't as good as they were, I would have been taken out by the fist that Ares sent flying in Marisol's direction. He landed his punch squarely on her nose, causing her head to snap back. There was a sickening crack, and I knew that her nose was broken.

"Clean her face and tie her back up," I instructed Bones as I wrapped my arm around my brother's shoulder and walked outside.

"How the fuck could she do something like that?" Ares asked as he paced the gravel parking lot. He punched at the air in anger. As I let him get his aggression out, I rolled him a blunt of some of the best hydro Miami had to offer.

"I can't tell you that, but I can tell you that you have to keep your emotions from clouding your judgment. We need to move smart if we plan on relaxing soon." I lit the blunt and took a pull before passing it to Ares.

"You're right. Here I was, thinking this bitch was a victim, and she played the fuck outta me. These bitches are making me weak."

"Don't think like that, bruh. The wrong bitch can make you weak. Marisol was definitely the wrong bitch. She is a lot like her father. They only care about their own motives. Now, Tori; she's a solid chick. If Zo says she's a good pick, then she's a good pick. I'm telling you now, bro, keep her around. She's good for you."

"She has to be," Ares said as he exhaled the potent weed. I could see his demeanor start to relax. "She got me turning down pussy and shit. I turned down Naomi's fine ass the other night at the club just to go home and climb into bed with Tori's ass."

"That's called growing up, bro. Plus, she's pregnant with yo' seed, so try to make that work. When this is all over, get yo' ass a real house and get out of that little ass condo."

"Shit, nigga, my shit is three bedrooms. Fuck I need all that room for?"

"You 'bout to be a family man. You gon' need the space. Trust me. I got a fucking mansion and still don't think I have enough space."

"I'm good where I am. I might turn one of those rooms into a nursery for my son, but we good over here."

"Son?" I chuckled. "I don't know why you and Titan think y'all having boys out the gate. Y'all niggas gon' have girls, just like my ass. They gon' drive y'all asses crazy and have your mean ass wrapped around their finger. You think Marisol had you acting out of character...wait until Tori pops out a girl on your ass. You gon' turn into some Barney ass nigga."

"What the fuck ever, nigga. You buggin'."

I laughed. Titan told me the same thing, but those niggas did not know what I knew. I had almost eight years in this to know. Niggas like us didn't get sons to carry on the name on the first try. Shit, it took me three tries to get me a little soldier. Don't get me wrong, my girls were some g's, but Apollo was who was gonna take over the throne when the time came.

My phone ringing cut our conversation short. I checked the caller

ID and instantly smiled because it was the call that I had been waiting on. Ares took a deep pull as he looked at me with a raised eyebrow. Sometimes, I forgot how much he looked like our father, Frank.

"I see you got the package I sent you," I said as I switched the phone to speakerphone.

"You're playing games you don't need to be playing now, DiBiasi," Francisco Santiago hissed into the phone.

"No. I don't think I am. We tried to come to a peaceful resolution, but you insist on being a pain in my ass, so you have to be dealt with accordingly."

My eyes traveled over to Ares, who was choking on his blunt as he laughed at my words. That nigga was clowning.

"You don't *deal* with me. Contrary to what you believe, Zeus, I am the sole ruler of Miami. You are operating on my turf."

"This is boring me. If you want your daughter back, the ball is in your court."

"So, what do you propose?"

"Let's have a sit down. I can go on forever, killing off your men one by one, but I want this shit to end. You and your crew come have a sit down with us. We will draw new territories so that everyone eats. We agree to not step on any toes, and we all win. Plus, you get your precious daughter back."

There was silence on the phone as Santiago considered my offer.

"Fine. Tomorrow at noon. Meet me at my warehouse in the everglades. ... I'm sure you know the one," he conceded.

"Done." I ended the call.

"You know you fucked up, right?" Ares asked with a smirk on his face. "Why would you meet him on his own turf?"

"It don't matter where we meet him. He's gon' meet his maker wherever we're at," I said with finality.

"Word," Ares agreed as he dropped the roach of his blunt and snuffed it out with his boot.

CHAPTER 17

Titan

"Time to roll in 'bout an hour, bruh," Zeus called out from the other side of the bedroom door.

We were all so amped about today that we decided to just crash at our condo since it was closer to Santiago's warehouse—all except Ares. My baby brother was so fucked up about Marisol that he needed to clear his head before we had what we intended to be a last stand with Santiago, so he dipped out to lay up under Tori.

Shit, even I was shocked that the bitch, Marisol, had got something like that over on Ares. Ares had some fucked-up ways when it came to dealing with his stable, but he always kept it one hundred with them; he always let 'em know exactly what was and wasn't gonna happen between them. He really started to have a soft spot for Marisol in light of what we now knew was a fake ass pregnancy, so I knew it cut my brother to the core. He didn't have to come out and say it, but I could tell that he was looking forward to having that kid.

Mama always said that, when we took a big loss, it was because the Lord was making way for something even better to come along, and it looked like that was exactly what was goin' down with Ares. I just hoped we could really dead this shit with Santiago for good so Tori wasn't the next casualty to get caught up in this war—I didn't even wanna begin to think about what Ares would do if something like that happened.

I tossed and turned all night, thinking about the move we had to make today. I wasn't nervous, but I was damn sure on edge. We had taken so many losses since Santiago had decided to make it his mission to bring the DiBiasi empire down, but the sense of resolve to bring this war to an end was urgent than a muthafucka for me—shit, for us all. Zeus had just welcomed his first son, Po was now my fiancée and mother-to-be to my firstborn, and even Ares' wild ass had a seed on the way. Our lives were all changing, our family tree was growing, our legacy was expanding, and that was some shit that we had to protect and preserve—by any means necessary.

My mind flipped back to how this shit with Santiago almost took us out before we even had a chance to make it to Cuba. If we didn't have thorough niggas like Bones and Knowledge on payroll, Zeus might have left this earth without ever meeting Apollo. That was some ill shit, and definitely something I never wanted to face now that I had a seed on the way.

Whatever happened, I knew life would never be the same once we headed out that door to this meeting with Santiago. That shit was swimming all through my head in the shower, and even now as I sat on the edge of the bed feeling like I had the weight of the world on my shoulders, I knew that we were right on the cusp of an explosive climax, and Miami would never be the same when it was all said and done. All I knew was that I was tired of sleeping here, there, and everywhere else. I was ready to be back in my own shit, in my own bed—and with my damn woman.

I had one leg in my pants when my phone started jumping on the nightstand, and I damn near tripped as I scrambled to answer it, thinking it was Po. I tried to get at her last night after we made it in, but she must have been asleep. Aside from work, Po was the main thing that kept me grounded nowadays, so I definitely needed to hear her voice before I headed into battle today. I was just a few hours away from being able to tell her that she could hop her ass on the next flight out and come home to daddy, and that shit had a nigga's dick jumpin' with excitement.

When I scrolled and saw that it was a message notification from the realtor I'd been working with, I put my phone to the side and finished getting dressed since it wasn't anything urgent. Danica had been helping me look at houses since Zeus and I had gotten back from Cuba, and though she'd been working her ass off to find properties that she thought would be a good fit, I probably hadn't been the best client. I had yet to make a showing, and I didn't feel bad about it. I knew she was on top of her shit and was, no doubt, putting in major work to earn a fat commission check, mainly because I saw how she helped India shut a slew of potential buyers out to snag the space for her second salon location. I just had so much other shit on my dome that buying a house was really the last thing I had time to be bothered with. I knew I had to deal with the shit eventually, though, especially if I wanted Po to give in and bring her ass back to Miami.

Danica had sent links to the full listings for five properties, one of which was right in Zeus' neighborhood. I swiped through the pictures real quick and had to admit that the house was bad, and with it being near Zo, I was sure Po would probably go for it. I shot Danica a quick text to schedule a showing and finished getting ready. I guess I'd try not to stand her up this time and make the effort to go see the house.

Po must have felt a nigga thinkin' about her because I couldn't even get my shirt on good before my phone was jumpin' again, this time with an incoming FaceTime call from her. I accepted the call and waited a few seconds for her to come into view, and damn! I got an eyeful at the sight of Po, her sisters, Cloryz and Yael, and my nieces, Perry and Athena.

"Heyyyyyy, Uncle Titan!" Athena sang the second she saw my face.

"Hey, boss lady!"

Though Athena was only a year older than her younger sister, Perry, she took her big sister duties to heart and was just as bossy as her mama. Zo always joked that she was six going on twenty-six.

"Auntie Po says I get to name one of the babies, and Perry can name the other, but I get to go first because I'm the oldest!" Athena continued.

"Is that right? Well, are you taking good care of your auntie for me?"

"Yup, but I got a bad report. She drank a soda today even though Mommy told her it was bad for the baby."

"Snitch!" Perry piped in. "Auntie Cloro said snitches get stitches!"

She frowned.

"Get out my conversation, Perry!" Athena clapped back, and it took everything in me not to fall out laughing. My nieces were a handful, and from what I saw, they were soaking up too much Orozco sauce being down there in Cuba.

"What's good, bae? Why y'all down there brainwashing them lil' girls?" I winked at Po.

"Not brainwashing—makin' sure we put them up on game while they're young so they don't get played by bums like you." Cloro smirked. She had a slick ass mouth and always had some smart shit to say, but it was all love.

"Right, because I can't have my nieces bringin' home no butter soft nigga like Dante."

Cloro shifted position so that she was now blocking my nieces' view of me then shot me a pair of birds while mouthing the words *fuck you* before Po pushed her out of the way.

"Y'all see me trying to have a conversation. Can you take all that noise somewhere else?" Po rolled her eyes before tossing a pillow at Yael, who was seated closest to her.

"You lucky you're pregnant, or you would catch this fade. It's cool, though. We'll leave so you can tell Titan about how you almost killed his babies," I heard Yael announce as the volume of her voice dropped, almost like she was moving further away.

"Bye, Uncle T!" my nieces cooed before I heard the door shut at their exit.

"The f—what's she talkin' about, Po?" I frowned, wishing we were having this conversation face to face because I knew damn well...

"Relax, T. I'm fine, and you know Yael is so extra. I went to yoga class with Ananda and tripped on som—"

"Why can't you just keep your ass somewhere with your feet up?"

"I'm pregnant, Titan, not disabled. You act like I'm supposed to stop living just because I'm having a baby. What's your problem? All I do is stay stuck up in this house every day while everyone else is living their lives without a care in the world. What about me? Nobody cares about me!" Po blurted, and I couldn't keep my facial expression in check even if I'd tried to.

What in the entire fuck just happened? She was just smiling and laughing, even joking with her crazy ass sister, so what the fuck? This must be that hormonal shit Zeus told me about that chicks be on when they were pregnant.

"Ma, believe me when I say that, outside of my mama, there ain't nothin' else I care about more than you and my seed. I just want you to be able to take time out and enjoy being catered to."

I tried to pull her out of the irrational tantrum she'd just thrown. Shit was funny, but I knew that if I even looked like I was about to laugh, I was gon' dive right into that drought Zeus warned me about.

"How 'bout you call and set something up at that spa that you and Zo alwa—"

I stopped right in my tracks and frowned when I realized the shit Yael and my niece had both said that slipped right past me. *Babies?*

160

"Hold up, what they mean *babies?*" I mumbled, and that shit seemed to work like magic because Po's pouty frown was immediately replaced with a smile so wide that I thought I could see her tonsils.

"Zo dragged me to the doctor after I fell, and they did a quick ultrasound just to make sure everything was okay with the baby, ... but they saw two babies."

"The fuck? How the hell is that possible? You just had a sonogram and ...the fuck?"

Two babies? Damn, this shit was crazy and had me seriously scratching my head. How the hell were we gonna take care of two infants at the same time? I swear I wasn't expecting this shit.

"The doctor said the second baby was probably hiding behind baby #1 and just didn't show up in that first sonogram."

I was still stuck on mute as my mind started racing through all the shit I had to do to get ready to bring two babies home. I now needed to find a house like ASAP!

"Titan? Say something ..."

"Umm, wow, bae. That's good shit! I mean, damn, two sons? You excited?"

"What makes you think you're getting even one son?" Po teased, wiping the smile slam off my face.

"Yo, we better not be having girls. We got enough women in the damn family."

"Maybe we are, and maybe we aren't, but you'll find out with everybody else at the gender reveal." Po winked and brought an envelope up into view—I guess the one that contained the sonogram images.

"Uh huh, well look, with two of my babies, you damn sure gon' bring your ass back here to deliver."

Two babies meant twice as much work, but twice as much chance that something could go wrong. I needed my babies born on U.S. soil with me.

"I don't know about that, Titan. Johanna has a friend that's a doula, and she was telling me about water birth, and I think that's something I want to try. It's less painful and puts less stress on the babies during labor. Papa is having someone come out tomorrow to take measurements to set up a birthing area for me. Cloro is taking me to look at birthing pools too."

"Po, you can have the babies wherever you want, as long as it's here. And we can get whatever pool you want as long as it's here."

As much as I loved Po, this was some shit that wasn't up for debate.

"Miami is gonna be our home base, Po, and this whole process of getting ready for the babies will be a lot easier if you're already settled and shit."

"Tell you what. I can agree to move there under two conditions. One, I gotta know my babies are gon' be safe, and I'm not tryin' to have to worry about whether you're going to make it home every night. And two, I get to pick the house."

"Already in progress, and done. That's all you want?" I smiled, knowing that, by this time tomorrow, we'd all be able to give our

162

families the all-clear to return to Miami. Yup, I definitely needed to make time to get up with Danica and see that house.

Po started babbling on about some other over-the-top shit she'd bought in celebration of finding out we were having twins, but I had to cut her off when I looked down at my watch and saw what time it was.

"Bae, me and Zeus gotta make a move right quick, so I gotta run. But I'm about to send you something I need you to look at. Check it out, and I'll hit you back in a few hours to see what you think. Oh, where's Zo?"

"Probably off somewhere nursing fatman. That baby is so damn greedy that Zo can barely unlatch long enough to pee in peace," Po laughed.

"Uh huh, well, you better watch and learn because you got two you gon' have to nurse, and I can't wait to see how you're about to juggle that shit."

Po did that little frowning thing she did when she was in deep thought, and I could see her wheels turning, as she was already thinking about how she was about to balance two babies.

"Aight, well, hug 'em for me both, and ay, make sure you check that thing out I'm 'bout to send you."

"Okay, T. Be careful, love you!"

"Yup." I nodded, forwarding the link for the house the minute our call disconnected.

"You done bein' all in love and shit?" Zeus' voice boomed.

"Ay, a nigga don't know shit 'til he been in love."

"No doubt, you know I know. Let's get to this business, though. I'm ready to get this shit over with."

Zeus led the way as we locked up and got ready to ride out. We decided to head to this meeting in different vehicles because the last thing we intended to do was let Santiago get one-up on us. He'd done nothing but disrespect our city since he showed up, tried to fuck up our money, shook our staff up, and had damn near backed us into a corner by making us send our families away. DiBiasis didn't run from shit, and it was time we let that muthafucka know once and for all that there was no room for him in Miami. This was our fuckin' city, and it always would be.

"Hold up, lemme take this right quick," I called after Zeus right as he stepped out the front door.

I'd been waiting on this call from Knowledge and didn't wanna wait for this info, because there was no telling what was about to go down at this warehouse. Knowledge was on the move and putting shit into place before Zeus even got off the phone with Santiago last night. I had no doubt that we were about to wreck some shit; there was just no telling how bloody it was about to get.

"Boss man, so check it. Everything's set up, but I took a break to check the set-up at ol' girl's spot. Ran the tape back, and it's mostly calls with her parents and home girls, but two conversations stood out. One was with that dude, Mondo …"

"The nigga that works for Santiago?"

"Yup, and the other one tripped me out. Sounded like her and another chick plottin' on how to get at you in your next house and shit."

"My next house? Nigga, I ain't got one house right now. The fuck you mean next?"

"The next house she's about to sell you. The other chick was your realtor, Danica."

What the fuck?

Ж

After a quick meet-up to run through our plans, we were on the move and heading into Santiago's territory. I was riding with Zeus, while Ares and Vinny rode together. Bones was gonna pull up solo, while Poody and Black, Ares' crew, were riding together, so we had a total of four vehicles headed into battle. We planned to set up a perimeter around the warehouse and have all points of access covered. Knowledge had what we called his Reflection Crew move out last night and set up surveillance so we could pull a live feed of Santiago's property. Them niggas were so efficient that the only sign they'd been in and out of your shit was the shadow they left behind, hence the *Reflection Crew.*

The surveillance had confirmed just what we expected: Santiago went to great lengths to set up the kind of ambush that would take out all of South Beach. Sadly, for him, he was about to fall into the same grave that he called himself digging for us.

"Yo, you good nigga?" Zeus probed since I'd been quiet the entire ride.

I just nodded my answer, still pondering the information Knowledge had just dropped on me about India. Every time I felt like I had just got a handle on things, here came some more shit to throw

165

a nigga off his square. I swear I didn't want this shit with India to end like this, but the bitch had quickly become one of those loose ends that Zeus was talking about. I didn't know if India had been this fraud all along, but that shit didn't even matter at this point. My heart was with Po, and I was committed to the DiBiasi empire, so India was a non-factor that had to be dealt with.

"Whatever it is, let that shit ride until we finish up here. We hope we're two steps ahead of Santiago, but we also gotta be prepared for the possibility that he got some snake shit up his sleeve. Either way, we need heads clear and eyes open. And you already know what to do if it comes down to it."

Zeus kept his eyes on the road and spoke with the reverence that he only got when we were headed into battle.

"And remember, if we don't make it home to call them Orozco sisters tonight, we're dead men anyway," Zeus joked, trying to lighten the mood.

"Real talk, bruh."

Pulling up into our designated spot, we waited for the other three vehicles to get into place before we made that move.

"This is what it's all about...the kinda shit Pops was always preparing us for," Zeus commented, drawing another nod from me.

"No doubt, and ain't shit to do but make him proud," I added.

Just then, Zeus' phone jumped with three messages in rapid succession, letting him know that the rest of our crew had arrived and was in place. Zeus and I gave each other one last look, leaned over to slip into a brotherly hug, and then exited the vehicle to get into place.

Less than a minute later, Vinny and Ares moved into position off to our left, while Poody and Black posted up off in the distance to our right. Bones was in position directly across from the spot where I stood, but on the opposite side of the building, so we couldn't see him.

Zeus turned his attention to Vinny and Ares, while I took Poody and Black. We affirmed our next steps with nods and subtle nonverbals, took them thangs off safety, and moved out. Poody and Black took off first, arriving at their next post with ease. Next were Vinny and Ares, and once they had advanced, Zeus and I took off. We were all crouched in the thick perimeter of bushes, the only cover afforded before we stepped out into the 360-degree strip of land that surrounded the warehouse. The feed from Knowledge's surveillance let us know that they planned to meet us in the front of the building while a crew was waiting at the rear of the building to loop around the exterior of the building and follow us in. We had something for them, though.

I turned to give Zeus one last look before we moved out, but my brother's stoic expression was replaced with one of panic when he lost his footing and went crashing face-first into the dusty earth.

"Shi—" Zeus attempted to exclaim, but his voice was cut short by the one thing we were hoping to avoid.

BOOM!

We felt the ground shudder beneath our feet, followed by a barrage of gunfire that made one thing crystal clear: we were in some deep shit now!

POW! POW! POW!

Just like that, we were met with a hail of rounds that were whizzing our way so quickly that we could feel the breeze left in their wake.

"Fuck! Move!" Zeus bellowed, sending the rest of our team into action.

I could now see that reason for his fall—an invisible tripwire—and helped him get his leg untangled so we could get the fuck up outta dodge. When I saw smoke coming from a top row of windows along the wall of the warehouse, I knew Bones had made his move and within minutes, the yard would be swarming with—make that thirty seconds.

"Yo, we got that side!" Vinny's voice rang out, and I shot him a glance to confirm his plan B.

I gave him a quick nod to let him know I'd heard him before turning my attention to Poody and Black. They were out in the open and unprotected, but busting them thangs and raining gunfire on each of Santiago's men as they fled the effects of the CS grenade that Bone's ass had set off indoors. Right then and there, I decided that I was gonna kick Bones's ass when we made it out this shit because that nigga ain't give us no warning about that fuckin' grenade. Thanks to him, everybody's sinuses were ripped open with tears and snot, slowing us down as we tried to clap back against this nigga, Santiago!

Zeus was on his feet with me, just mere inches behind, as we took out a cluster of dudes headed in Ares and Vinny's direction.

POW! POW!

I felt some shit nick my ear before I whipped around and blasted a hole through some George Lopez lookin' muthafucka that to tried sneak up behind Zeus and me.

"Not today, muthafucka!" my voice boomed.

Between Vinny, Ares, Poody, Black, Zeus, and me, that yard was lit the fuck up like a fireworks display on the Fourth of July. Each time one of Santiago's men ran up, we met 'em with some special rounds that we reserved just for shit like this. The rounds were coated with a special protectant that kept them intact until they made contact with their target. Upon entry, the rounds bounced around in the body cavity for a few seconds before separating, basically exploding the body from the inside out.

A good five minutes passed before we found ourselves standing in a graveyard of fetid body parts and partial corpses. Bones had yet to appear, and I was hoping he had used the last of his grenades because I was just starting to feel like I could breathe clearly. Zeus and I had separated at this point, with him flanking the building to the right, while I took the left. Vinny and Ares quickly came into view and tossed questioning looks over their shoulders to assess my condition. Seeing that I was unharmed and still on the move, they nodded and shifted focus back to whatever was in front of them. I caught sight of a side entrance to the building and was just about to head that way when—

"Ahhhhhhhh shit!"

Zeus' voice rang out, and I felt my veins go ice cold with terror at hearing the sound a nigga never wanted to hear from his blood. I retraced my steps on autopilot, racing out to the open yard to see why the fuck my brother was sounding off. I had no idea what I was about to walk up on, and I slipped into an instant bargain with the Lord that if he spared me the shock that I really didn't want to walk up on, I'd do a better job of making it to mass on the regular. I also begged him to let me not walk up on that kind of shock because, if I did, I could kiss all hopes of seeing my twins come into the world goodbye because Zo would take my fuckin' head off!

CHAPTER 18

Ares

$\mathcal{S}$hit around me was hectic, but my focus was getting inside of the warehouse to off Santiago's bitch ass. His men were falling down around us left and right, so it wouldn't take much more for me to make it on the inside. I looked over at Vinny, who had a big grin on his face. He couldn't even hide the excitement that killing gave him, but I'd be lying if I said I wasn't just as excited. Well, maybe I was a little less excited 'cause my main reason for wanting to kill him was a lie.

Finding out that Marisol was never pregnant hurt me to the core. I was going out of my way trying to make sure her ass was alright, when nothing was wrong with her in the first place. The small piece of me that once cared about her didn't give two shits about her dying now. She tried to play me, but ended up playing herself in the long run. Even with the games she played with me, I couldn't bring myself to squeeze the trigger on her. Vinny had no problem with it, of course, so he put a bullet right between her eyes for me.

When I saw Santiago's fat, pudgy ass running toward his car, I knew that my chance to kill him had finally come. My heart was racing

171

uncontrollably at the sight of his fat ass. As soon as I started his way, I heard Zeus scream out in pain. I looked in the direction that I heard the howl coming from, and I saw Titan rushing over to check it out. The sound he let out wasn't a good one, so my first instinct was to go check on my brother. Titan waved me off and pointed toward Santiago, who was jumping into his getaway car.

"Cover me!" I shouted at Vinny right before taking off toward Santiago.

The car engine purred, then the wheels started kicking up dirt, trying to make its escape.

POW! POW! POW!

Three shot rang out simultaneously, sending bullets flying past me and into the tires of the getaway car. The car began to fishtail, then it flipped over twice before coming to rest on its hood. I was sprinting toward the car as fast as I could, and I could hear footsteps galloping behind me. I figured that it was Vinny, but I was so focused on getting to Santiago that I didn't even turn around to confirm it. The fact that no one was shooting at me gave me confidence that it was Vinny.

Just as Vinny and I made it to the back of the car, I heard a car engine roar, then peel out. I looked back to see Titan speeding toward the exit. Something must've happened for him to leave us out here like this. I had to take care of Santiago quick so that I could find out what happened. I approached the car slowly with my finger on the trigger, waiting to let loose. Smoke and dust were everywhere, so I didn't have a clear view of what was in front of me. Vinny crept up behind me, and I signaled for him to go to the driver side to make sure that the driver was dead while I approached the passenger side. I could hear moaning, so someone inside of the car was sure enough live. The dust was just beginning to clear out when I hear two shots come from Vinny's side of the car. Vinny didn't waste any time putting bullets in the driver. Unlike Vinny, I wanted to fuck with Santiago before I sent him to meet his maker. I needed to let him know to his face that he lost this war.

I looked down and saw Santiago lying there looking back at me. His hand was hanging out of the broken window, so I grabbed it and pulled his ass out of the car. He laid there laughing, but keeping his gaze locked on me. Since he was laughing, I put a smile on my face.

"So, we meet again," I joked.

"Fuck you!"

Oh, this muthafucka gon' talk shit instead of pleading for his life? I don't blame him, though; if I was about to die, I would go out like a man too. Ain't no needing in bitching up, especially when you know that it is over. At least the fat bastard got heart.

"I'll pass, I like to fuck women. Marisol didn't tell you?"

"Where is my daughter?" he spat.

"Umm, I guess she's in heaven. That is, if her lyin', back stabbin' ass repented before she took one to the dome."

He started rattling off something in Spanish while Vinny and I stood over him laughing. That's when I saw the tears building up in his eyes. I knew that would be a hard pill for him to swallow; that's why I said it. He didn't give a fuck about us killing him because he knew that this day would come. I knew the only way to hurt him at this point was to tell him that Marisol was dead.

"Ares, stop playin' with this muthafucka, we gotta go," Vinny barked.

That brought me back to reality, and I remembered that my brothers raced out of here a few minutes ago. I squatted down next to Santiago so that I could look him right in his eyes.

"Checkmate, fat BITCH!"

POW! POW!

I let two go into the side of his head, then Vinny pulled me up by my shirt and dragged me toward the car. Once I was able to catch my balance, I took off full speed, passing Vinny with the quickness.

The first thing I did when we jumped into the car was grab my phone. I had ten missed calls from Titan, and a text from Black.

Black: *Meet us at Ryder*

I pressed the button to call him while burning rubber to get far away from this place. The phone rung once before Black picked up.

"What the fuck, bro!"

"Man, it's Zeus. He got shot."

"What! Is he okay?"

"We just now pullin' up to the hospital. I'm behind Titan, so I don't know yet, but he wasn't lookin' too good when we got him into the car."

"Fuuuuck!" I shrieked. "I'll be there in a minute."

I hit the gas, causing both me and Vinny's heads to fly back into the headrest.

"What happened?" Vinny questioned, grabbing for his seatbelt.

"Zeus is shot. Black said he wasn't lookin' too good."

"Damn," Vinny groaned.

Damn was right. Who the fuck is gonna call Zo's crazy ass and tell her that Zeus got shot? It damn sure couldn't be me because she was going to flip out, and I didn't want to flip out right back on her ass. I didn't feel like fighting all them Cuban bitches over no dumb shit.

I flew into the hospital parking lot and jumped out of the car. Vinny jumped into the driver's seat to go find a parking space. Black was waiting on me at the door, so I jogged toward him.

"What's the deal?"

"They took him in for emergency surgery."

"Where's Titan?"

"He's upstairs in the waiting room. Go to the second floor, I'll wait right here for Vinny."

"A'ight, bro."

"Y'all get 'em?"

I directed my eyes down to my shirt that had blood splattered on it, "What you think?"

"Cool," he let out a sigh of relief.

I raced inside of the hospital, headed in the direction of the elevators. One just so happened to open, so I slipped inside and pressed the two button.

It was just one floor up, but it felt like it took forever for me to get to the second floor. As soon as the elevator doors opened, I ran out in search of Titan. I saw Knowledge standing against a wall, so I knew that Titan had to be in the vicinity. Knowledge looked up and saw me coming, then Titan stepped from behind the wall.

"What it look like?" I asked before I could even make it to them.

"I don't know, bro," Titan answered. "Shit wasn't lookin' good."

"Why y'all keep sayin' that!? Was he alive when y'all got here!?"

"Yeah nigga, and stop yellin' at me."

"Who called Zo?"

"Bones went to call her. I don't feel like hearin' her mouth right now. I already know that Po is gon' call me with the shit."

"I'm callin' Mama." I began to pat my pockets, and that's when I remembered that I left my phone in the cup holder of the car. "Damn. I'll be right back."

As I trotted toward the elevator, Black and Vinny stepped off of it. Vinny held my phone up, and it started to sound off. I grabbed the phone away from him to look at the caller ID. It was my mama, so I pressed the button to answer.

"Ares!" she cried through the phone. "Wha-how? Oh God. How is my baby?"

I could hear all kinds of noise in the background of her phone; sounded like a war was going on behind her.

"Mama, calm down and breathe. Zeus is in surgery now, so we don't know anything."

"I need to be there, Ares. I need to be there with my baby."

176

"Okay, no problem. I'll get the pilot in the air for you."

"Alright. Are you okay?"

"Yes ma'am."

"And what about Titan?"

"He's fine, Ma."

"Thank goodness."

"Go get packed, Ma, and I'll see you soon."

"Okay, baby. I love you."

"I love you too, Mama."

I couldn't even hang up from my mama good before Tori was ringing my phone. She must've heard something for her to be calling because she knew that we were handling business today.

"Hey."

"Ares, are you okay?"

"Yeah."

She started crying. "Baby, I just want you to come home with me."

"Stop cryin'. I can't come right now, Zeus got shot."

"What? Where are you?"

"Ryder."

"I'm on my way."

Before I could tell her not to come, she hung up in my face. I didn't want her here with all this commotion going on, but at the same time, I did want her here by my side. I needed her comfort to take my mind off Zeus, even if just for a minute.

Ж

Hours had gone by, and we were still sitting in the waiting room hoping for news about Zeus. A few times, a surgeon came out to let us know that they were still working on him. It didn't put me at ease, but the fact that they were still working on him meant that he was still alive. While Tori sat beside me rubbing the top of my head, I thought back to when we were children. I thought about when Zeus taught me how to ride a bike. I was like four years old, but I remember it as clear as day. How could I forget? I scraped my legs and knees up a hundred times before I finally got it. Titan stood off to the side making fun of me, but Zeus was patient enough to keep showing me until I got it right.

Although I give him hell every chance I get, I admired Zeus in so many ways. He was the first to get married and start a family, showing us that monogamy was possible. If y'all think I'm terrible, you should have known Zeus before Zo made him sit the fuck down. Dude stayed hitting chicks all over Miami on a daily basis. The only reason he stopped was because Zo caught him with a bitch, killed her, and announced that she was pregnant. Tori was like Zo in many ways, though I doubt if she's killed anyone. She was strong enough to deal with the shit that the DiBiasis had going on, and she was still willing to stick around. Tori was definitely stronger than any of the other chicks I've dealt with before. She didn't back down from me often, and she didn't let my sarcasm stop her from loving me. I needed her in my life to put me in check when I'm actin' an ass for no reason. I just hope that she got along well with my mama, Zo, and Po.

"Tori."

"Huh?"

"Are you happy?"

"Yes," she said, pushing my forehead back so that she could look me in my eyes. "You scare me a lot, but I am happy with you."

"How do I scare you?"

"This," she complained, looking around the waiting room with her eyes. "I don't want to be out here waitin' to hear news about you."

"It's over, baby. It's all over."

"Good, because we can't survive without you. Me and little Tatianna need our daddy."

"Don't do that. Don't wish no girl on me. And I'm gon' be here for Lil' A 'til he's grown."

"I want a mini me," she whined.

"Hell nah, I don't need two of yo' ass walkin' around my house talkin' shit."

"You better get ready," she joked.

"I'm for real, babe. If we have a daughter, I know I will go crazy, especially if she is built like you."

"Oh, she will be. My mama is built just like this."

"Shit."

She laughed. "Speakin' of which, she wants to meet you."

"Okay."

That shit made her light up like a Christmas tree. Girls like for you to meet their parents; I guess that makes shit official for them. I was ready to make shit official, so it was time for me to finally meet her mother and for her to meet mine. I mean, we were having a baby, for goodness sake.

The surgeon finally emerged from behind the OR doors, heading in our direction. We all stood up and started toward him, meeting him halfway.

"Mr. DiBiasi survived surgery, but things are still touch and go. Right now, he is in a medically induced coma..."

When I heard the word coma, my knees damned near gave out on me. A coma was as close you as you could get to death. The doctor was still talking, but I hadn't heard a word he said after *coma*. The last thing I wanted for my brother was for him to become a damn vegetable. It ain't right for a person to have to live like that.

"Will he come out of it?" Titan questioned.

"We don't know, we have to wait and see what happens in the next few hours."

"Can we see him?" I asked.

"They're taking him to ICU on the fifth floor. You can wait up there, and once he is situated, we'll come get you."

We didn't waste any time stampeding toward the elevator to go up a few floors. Though we still had to wait, we were in a rush to get up there. I was ready to get home and get out of these bloody clothes, but I couldn't leave here without laying eyes on my brother first. If I could just see his face, I think I would be able to get through the night.

CHAPTER 19

Zeus

(As Told by Xiomara "Zo" DiBiasi)

*M*y heart beat at the steady click of my heels as I marched down the sterile hospital hallway. I had the driver bring me straight from the airport after a very tense plane ride. I held hands with my mother in law, Eva, and prayed for my husband. I knew that Titan and Ares avoided calling me because they thought I was crazy and I would go off, but they were wrong. Zeus had always prepared me for this day.

As intimidating and invincible as my husband was, he always prepared me for the day when the streets would take him away from me. We were born into this, so it wasn't like there was an easy out. We couldn't just clean up our money and bow out like many of these self-proclaimed street kings. This shit was inherited, and we carried the responsibility of keeping the family business alive until our children were old enough to take over. I dreaded the thought because my babies were still so young and innocent, but soon, they would begin their training just as Zeus and I had.

Finally making it to my destination, I pushed open the doors marked Intensive Care Unit. I almost ran smack into Bones as I hurried through the door with Eva on my heels. Bones stood to the side as he pointed me in the direction of Titan and Ares. I could see the dread on their faces as I approached. I didn't give a fuck. I was glad that they thought I was crazy.

"Where is he?" I asked, dismissing their looks of dismay.

"He's in room 513. There can only be two people back there at a time," Titan spoke up. I nodded and grabbed Eva's hand as we did the slow funeral march through the doors marked *Patient Rooms*.

When I entered his room, I had to stifle a sob. Zeus would not want me to be a weak bitch, but he was my heart. I felt like the walls were closing in on me as I looked at my husband hooked up to several machines. Honestly, I would have expected Ares to take a bullet before Zeus. Sure, he had his wild ways before we got married, but Zeus was always so levelheaded and calculating. He could see ten steps ahead of the average person.

"*Dios mío,*" Eva whispered as soon as she laid eyes on Zeus.

He was swollen. He did not even look like himself. I could tell by the many bandages that he had been shot several times. The bandage around his head and jaw was what stood out the most to me. I choked back another sob at the realization that the love of my life was in a more serious condition than I had anticipated.

"Z," I whispered to him as I stepped up to him. "I'm here, Z. I need you to fight this. I know you tried to prepare me for this day, but

I'm not ready to let you go just yet. We got the babies to think about. You need to be here for your son. He barely knows his father."

At that point, I couldn't contain my composure as tears slipped from my eyes. I wanted to scream at him. How dare he think it was okay to leave me?

"Zeus, if you die, I will bring you back to kill you. Do you hear me? You better fight through this," I whispered harshly before kissing his bandaged cheek and leaving Eva with her eldest son.

I clutched my rosary as I walked back to the waiting room. Ares and Titan were seated, and it looked like the weight of the world was on their shoulders. I did not blame them. I knew they thought I did, but Zeus was the oldest. He was their leader, older brother, and role model. I knew they were taking this hit just as hard as I was.

"What happened, T?" I asked quietly, taking a seat beside my brother-in-law.

"I don't know, Zo. We knew we were walking into an ambush and were prepared for it," he began to explain. "They had the place rigged with booby traps, and Zeus inadvertently alerted them to our position when he tripped over the invisible tripwire. We recovered okay and were able to take out the majority of Santiago's crew. I took my eyes off of him for a split second to direct our team. Then, I heard him scream in front of me. I had never heard that sound come from him, man."

Titan shuddered and a tear slipped from his eye. I grabbed his hand tightly. I did not want to sound insensitive to his pain because I knew that we all were hurting, but I did not want my husband's possible death to be in vain if the mission wasn't completed.

"Did you get Santiago?" I asked softly.

"Hell yeah. I sent that fat fuck to hell, where he belongs," Ares spat venomously.

A smile graced my lips. "Good. All of this was not in vain. This was war. There were going to be casualties. We need to pray that he pulls through this. Has anyone contacted Father Rossi?" I asked them, referring to our family's priest.

They both shook their heads. I chuckled a bit because I already knew why they were avoiding Father Rossi. I was sure neither of them nor my husband had been to confession since this whole mess had started. I pulled my phone out to dial his number. Before I could bring it up to my ears, a heart wrenching scream shook me to my core.

"Ma?" Titan and Ares said simultaneously. They both stood to their feet and headed back toward the double doors that led to the room with me hot on their heels. Once the doors opened, doctors and nurses were rushing into Zeus' room from every direction. The chaos caused my heart rate to speed up as I got closer to his room.

"Ma'am, you can't be back here," I heard one of the nurses trying to get Eva out of the room.

"That's my son! I have to be here!" she protested.

"Yo, get yo' hands off of my mama before I peel yo' cap back!" Ares caught up to the nurse that was trying to hold back a hysterical Eva.

"Calm down! This is not good for the patient. I need everyone to step back and let us do our jobs!" a doctor yelled over all of the commotion in an effort to get us to calm down.

The monitors were going crazy, and I wanted to get a better look. When I walked closer to the room, nothing could prepare me for what I saw. Zeus was convulsing. The seizures were so severe that it looked like his spirit was trying to separate from his body. I watched in terror as the doctors were finally able to sedate him.

"I have to call Father Rossi," I mumbled. I didn't know what I was calling him for, though. I didn't know if I was calling him to read Zeus' last rites or to pray for a miracle.

Ж

Three Weeks Later...

They told me that my survival was a miracle. People didn't come back from injuries like mine. They didn't heal as quickly as I did. I told them that I was named Zeus for a reason.

"Are you comfortable?" Zo asked as she fluffed the pillow behind my head. She hadn't left my side since I had opened my eyes two days ago, and I wanted her to get some rest.

I nodded as much as my stiff neck would allow me to. I had been shot twice in my chest and in my thigh. Doctors told me that if one of the bullets had been about two inches lower, it would have hit my heart and I would have died.

"You don't have to do this. Get some rest. Go spend some time with the kids," I urged Zo. Po and Cloryz brought them up from Cuba since Zo didn't want to leave my side.

"The kids are fine. They are ready for you to get better so that they can see you. You know they don't allow kids in the ICU," Zo fussed.

"What? I want to see my kids. I have enough money to buy this fucking ICU. Yo, call your sisters and tell them to bring my kids to me."

"Okay, babe, I'll be right back."

Zo smiled before she left the room. There was hope in her eyes that I was returning to the old me. The truth was that I had never left. I was not going to let a few bullets keep me from being there for my family. They would have to do a lot worse than that.

"Your wife told me you were back here raising hell," Titan said as he entered the room. He had a devilish smirk on his face.

"I ain't doing shit. I'm tired of the muthafuckas telling me who can and can't visit me when I can pay their salary plus some. Shit, I want to see my damn kids."

"I can dig it."

"Fuck you doing up here anyway? I thought you would be laid up in some pregnant pussy right now."

"Man, Po's emotional ass won't even let me touch her. She's back on that *I got her pregnant on purpose* shit."

"Well nigga, did you?"

"Hell nah. I mean, I wasn't trying to prevent that shit either. Po has always been it for me. She just didn't see it."

"Because you were running up in everything with a pussy, nigga." I chuckled, causing a pain to shoot through my body.

"You're one to talk," Titan shot back.

"Yeah, I did my shit, but I slowed that shit all the way down when Zo shot Snow. I couldn't have my baby stacking up bodies because I was being reckless with the dick. Shit, I would've been next anyway."

"You damn right. Her and her crazy ass sisters would have had you hanging by your toenails or some shit while they used your ass for target practice," Titan said while laughing.

I laughed at the thought, but he was right.

"So, you ready for this marriage thing?" I asked, changing the subject and getting serious with my brother.

"I think I am. I'm ready to be like my big bro, you know? Settle down with Po and have more kids. Ain't shit out here but hoes anyway. Po wants more than my money, even though she is spending the hell out of my shit."

"You right, but she is also gon' help you make it back. As crazy as those sisters are, they are true ride or die women. You need to dead that shit with India for good too. Don't leave her ass around here lurking. It only opens you and Po up to her harassing y'all. You won't live in peace until you put her in her place," I preached.

"I know. I'm working on that as we speak. India won't be a problem for us, but your ass will if you don't hurry up and get better. Zo's ass won't let us have a wedding without you there. Shit, I don't want to have a wedding without you there. You my best man and shit, nigga."

"I thought I was yo' fucking best man," Ares' loud ass interrupted our conversation.

"This nigga," Titan said with a roll of his eyes.

"Yeah, *this* nigga. What the fuck, T? I thought I was yo' best man and shit," Ares joked.

"Nigga, you the best man to fuck some shit up. You the best man in charge of the bachelor party. I know you know some big booty strippers," Titan egged him on.

"Man, what the fuck ever. You ain't getting me shot up by Po." Ares waved him off.

"She ain't got to know," Titan countered.

"Shit, yo' ass gon' get married next," I pressed Ares. "I see how you been curving other bitches for Tori."

"You might be right, but we gon' see how this shit go. I'mma ask her to move in first. You know how some bitches get to acting funny when they have babies by you and shit," Ares confessed.

"You love that girl. Stop trying to act like you don't. You know Mama is not gon' like you bringing a baby into the world and not making an honest woman of Tori," Titan chided.

"Shit, Mama can marry her ass then. I'm just now getting to the point that I ain't fucking a different bitch every day. I'm taking baby steps, nigga," Ares grumbled.

I chuckled. There was hope for my baby brother. We chopped it up for a little while longer until Zo returned with the kids. She dropped ten stacks on each nurse and the reception desk to allow all three of my babies back to see me. I smirked because money talked over everything.

"Daddy!" Athena was the first in the room. She was followed closely by Perry, who had her thumb in her mouth.

"Hey, my princesses!" I greeted them with the widest smile my tired body could muster.

They each ran up to me to get a hug. Zo helped them into the bed with me.

"Daddy, when are you coming home?" Perry asked.

"I don't know yet, sweetie. Why?" I replied.

"Because ... Thena is being mean, and she won't let me play with my brother," she whined.

"No, I'm not!" Athena protested. "She's too little. I told her she needs to be bigger to hold him."

I laughed because Athena wasn't much bigger than Perry, but she swore she ruled her.

"Don't y'all come in here arguing, chicas. I already told y'all. See Zeus, I told you this was a bad idea," Zo warned.

"Nonsense. They're fine. They're no different than you and your sisters." I chuckled. "Hand me my boy," I demanded, holding out my arms for her to place Baby Apollo into them.

I smiled as soon as I laid eyes on my baby boy. He was the spitting image of me. I couldn't wait to buy him his first .380. My little nigga was gon' be a savage. He must have felt my presence because he opened his eyes wide, and a slight grin formed on his face.

"Yo, my little nigga just smiled at me," I gushed. If no one else could, my kids always turned me into a pile of mush.

"Nigga, that's just gas." Zo chuckled.

"Whatever. I know a smile when I see one."

I stared around me and soaked in my family. I needed to get better for them and my brothers because I did not want to miss moments like this. Hopefully, I would be released in a couple of weeks so that I could enjoy a Santiago-free existence. From what had been reported to me by Bones, Titan, and Ares, things had been running smoother than ever, and with the new protocol that Titan had put in place, our shit mirrored the shit that Dante had going on in Cuba. Shit was looking up, and I wanted to be around to reap the benefits.

CHAPTER 20

Titan

"This shit is about to be live, cuz," Vinny boasted. Anything that involved death had this nigga as excited as a side chick that fucked around and guessed the password to her dude's phone.

Shit had been crazy the past few weeks for us all. Zeus was driving Zo up a wall because he was tired of being laid up and was ready to get back to the family business with Ares and me. Zo wasn't having it, though, and she was on him like a hawk, making sure that he was taking it easy and allowing himself to fully recover like the doctors ordered. If it wasn't something he could handle with a few quick swipes or texts, it wasn't going down on Zo's watch.

Needless to say, I quickly realized just how much we needed Zeus in our day to day operations. I still had Vinny, though, and he'd been something of a godsend. He had more of a knack for the business side of things than I ever realized, and he even joked about snatching up a small spot to make Miami like a second home for himself. Vinny had gone above and beyond to make sure we were all straight during his stay, and with his return flight scheduled to leave tonight, I had to let him take this ride with me to handle one last order of business that was right up his alley.

"First Ares, and now you? Man, we have scandalous chicks up north, but these bitches down here take fraud to a whole new level," Vinny mumbled. "It's all good, though, because my partner is an equal opportunity banger, and she damn sure don't discriminate." *His partner,* as he affectionately called her, was the Hudson H9 his girl gifted him with for Sweetest Day a few years back. All the firepower he had in his arsenal, and she was a hands-down favorite.

I was still trippin' off the fact that I found myself in damn near an identical dilemma as the one Ares faced a few weeks back: learning that a bitch had no loyalty to a nigga or his dick. True enough, India probably had a long list of reasons to want to get at me, but she could've been more adult about the whole situation and let shit unload to my face. Aside from the fact that she'd burned down some shit that didn't belong to her, her *Waiting to Exhale* tantrum took an innocent life, and that was some shit that still had me tossing and turning at night. Nothing could ever make up for Taylor dying on my watch; add that to the fact that India was really on some scandalous shit and was still trying to get at me through Danica, her counterfeit realtor, and yeah—I had more than a few reasons to do what I knew had to be done.

Danica looked 'bout ready to shit bricks when I confronted her ass about her involvement in India's revenge plot. I wasn't sure what I was expecting, but her ass folded like a deck of cards and gave me a full rundown of just how far India was planning to take this get-back shit; good for me because it let me know exactly how I needed to cut the snake off at the head, but bad for Danica because she quickly became one of those *loose ends* that Zeus had been on us to take care of.

I figured India would be on edge and take extra care and caution in her moves, especially if she'd already figured out that Danica's ass was missing, so I had to come up with a foolproof way to lure her out into the open. All snake shit aside, India was about her business, which was why today's meeting would be the perfect cover for the shit I had planned. Not even a good twenty minutes after receiving the evite, she had RSVP'd and unknowingly signed her own death warrant. Knowledge had cooked up a fake VIP event for the beauty industry, then arranged for India to receive a fake evite, under the guise of some venture capital guru, requesting a one-on-one with her. She thought she'd be walking into an exclusive meeting to discuss a plan to franchise her salon/spa brand, but I had a trick for that ass.

"Okay, so check it. I need this shit to look and feel legit until the very last second. We have the whole building to ourselves for the next few hours, so that should be enough time to handle business, get the clean-up crew in, and make sure we leave the spot in the same condition we got it in. Brad is like family, and I'm not tryin' to beef with that nigga because we fucked his shit up," I explained just as we pulled up to delivery entrance of Red, the Steakhouse.

Knowledge had arranged for a car service—aka the *Reflection Crew*—to deliver India to the restaurant, and checking my watch, I saw that she should be pulling up any minute and decided to hang back for a few minutes to let her get seated and settled.

"Just so I'm clear, how messy is too messy up in this fine

establishment?" Vinny joked.

You'd think that he got his fill of dealing a healthy dose of death after that fuckin' massacre at Santiago's spot, but shit, this nigga's dick was still hard for some action, which let me know we had to get him the fuck up out of Miami before he got our ass tangled up in more shit like the mess we just put to rest with Santiago.

"A drop of blood is too messy, and I need her gone before she can complete a blink of her eyes."

Pissed as I was with India, I just couldn't bring myself to be the one that pulled the trigger. Don't get me wrong, I had no qualms about killing a bitch if the shoe fit, but with my firstborn babies on the way, I felt like I needed to sit this one out. I didn't need that kinda bad karma in my life. I planned to be close enough to see that *oh shit* realization just before her eyes went dark, but far back enough to dodge even a hint of her blood's spatter.

Five minutes later, my phone buzzed with a text from the maître d, confirming that India was in place, which meant it was go time.

"Let's get it," I gave Vinny the green light as I killed the engine, armed the alarm, and led us through the back entrance.

You'd never guess that this five-star restaurant was closed for business at the moment because the kitchen was abuzz like it was business as usual. I dapped Peter, one of the best chefs to ever do it, as we breezed through and made our entrance into the dining area. Knowledge had arranged for India to be seated in a private dining area that branched off from the main serving floor, so I slid into a tiny room that served as an observatory and allowed the wait staff to keep tabs on the patrons without excessively disturbing their dining experience.

Just like I knew she would, India dressed in her best and was serving up a heaping helping of cleavage in what she'd affectionately dubbed her *seal the deal* heels. She said they were good luck and an essential item in her kit to ensure successful business transactions, particularly when there was a dick present during negotiations. She'd just finished checking her face in a small compact when Vinny stepped in and joined her in the private room.

"Ms. Simon, so glad you could make it," Vinny announced his presence, and if I hadn't seen it with my own eyes, I wouldn't have believed it. My cousin—the Italian stallion, the man whose thirst for blood bordered on a twisted cannibalistic nature—had transformed into a polished and refined businessman right before my eyes.

"Mr. Marrone?" India rose to return his salutation.

"In the flesh, but call me Nic," Vinny owned the alias that Knowledge had created as I eavesdropped on what would be India's last meal. Sadly, she'd never even make it to the main course.

A few members of the wait staff moved in to remove their soup setting and set the salad course before them, and I got lost in thoughts of India for a hot minute. She had this fire about her that turned me on when we first met, and I guess that was what had sucked me in. There was a time when she let me do me, knew her place, and knew when to insert herself into my world to fuck me to a stress-free place. I never saw this woman scorned shit coming, and that let me know just how much trying to juggle her and Po had thrown me off my square. Zo didn't come out and say it, but I knew she was thinking that same *I told you so* that I should have taken heed of a long time ago. All I knew was that India had gone too far, and I'd be damned if I let Po or my babies get caught up in some bullshit that I intended to dead today, right here and now.

"So Nic, I did a little digging of my own, and Polaris Capital has an impressive portfolio. You guys have some pretty big names to boast. So, why me?" India shifted into business mode.

"I think you're asking the wrong question, Ms. Simon. A more appropriate inquiry would be why *not* you? Make no mistake, my company thrives on taking chances, but a man can never go wrong in taking a chance on a sure thing. That sure thing is beauty, specifically medical spas. Vanity just might be the new cardinal sin, and there's a lot of money to be made. My firm intends to do that with a brand that commands respect and can hold its own."

This nigga Vinny sounded like a fuckin' infomercial and shit! India fell quiet, no doubt mulling over his words before she spoke again.

"Respect. That's something I'm big on. I'll admit that you have my interest, Nic, but I'm a bit leery of franchising. I have very specific aspirations for my business, and I'm not interested in becoming lost in your corporate shuffle or being forced to change to fit a mold of what you believe is marketable."

"Understood, and you have my word that Polaris isn't interested in changing your business, so to speak. We're looking to help you become the industry standard in medical spa treatments. You will be the mold that your competition scrambles to emulate," Vinny affirmed.

"That sounds like something I can work with, so what do you need from me to transition into the next step?" India forked a small sample of the salad into her mouth, breaching those same lips that had sucked me dry many a night.

"I'm so glad you asked." Vinny raised his glass and swirled the crimson liquid before taking a sip—the signal we'd agreed on earlier that alerted me that I could make my entrance. I took a deep breath, adjusted my blazer, and joined in them in the private dining area to share one last conversation with India.

"There's just one last thing I'd like to address before we move into the main course," Vinny declared as my footsteps fell off just two feet short of their table. India brought her eyes up to observe what she'd assumed was the wait staff, but choked on her water as realization set in. She opened her mouth and did her best to form the words for her next statement, but her voice hadn't caught up.

"Sup, girl? Long time no see... look like you seen a ghost or somethin'...you aight?"

I stood with my hands loosely clasped in front of me, eager to get this shit over with.

"Titan, look. I know it looks bad, but I can explain," she finally found her voice.

"You're right; it does look bad … but not as bad as this." I smiled and in half a second, Vinny's partner made her appearance and sent a hot one right between those same bedroom eyes that India had seduced me with time and time again. She took her last breath with a permanent look of shock planted on her face as she fell head-first into the half-eaten salad set before her.

"That clean enough for you?" Vinny frowned, no doubt upset he didn't get to turn up a little more on this particular kill.

"Just what I had in mind. Good lookin' out, cousin. Knowledge just pulled up with a cleanup crew, so make sure they clear all this shit out so my man Brad can get back to business as usual. You can ride with Knowledge back to the shower because I gotta make a run right quick," I advised.

"I got you, T." Vinny dapped me as he got to his feet and crossed the floor to meet up with Knowledge, who had just joined us in the private dining room.

Minutes later, I was pulling away from the restaurant and breathing a little easier now that my last loose end had been taken care of. I had two stops to make before heading back to Zeus and Zo's house for the baby shower, so I burned rubber because I wasn't trying to show up late and hear Po bitchin' about my tardiness until she gave birth.

Ж

"Congratulations, Mr. DiBiasi; you're officially a homeowner … again," Pilar beamed. She was a realtor Zeus put me in touch with once I found out that Danica and India called themselves plotting. Pilar was able to convince the owners to terminate services with their previous firm and bring their business to her, ensuring she'd pull a fat commission out of the deal.

"You did good, and this is really gonna be the icing on the cake, Titan." Zo smiled, patting me on the back as she ventured further into the home to give herself another tour.

Po knew about this house, but she didn't know that it was *her* house per se. I scooped her, Cloro, my nieces, and Mama up one day under the guise of finding a new spot for Mama that would allow her to be closer and readily accessible to Zo now that she was juggling three kids. Turned out that it was one of Po's good days with no bipolar pregnancy hormones causing her to act an ass, so she was all smiles at the thought of house shopping. The minute she walked through the door, her face lit up. She kept a big ass Kool-Aid smile the entire time, and when we got to the end of the showing, Mama asked Po what she thought. That was when the waterworks started, and I thought *oh shit, here we go!* Po surprised us all, though, and gushed over how amazing the house was. That sealed the deal for me, so I shot Pilar a text at that very moment and told her to close the deal and get the paperwork ready for my signature.

"Shit, I hope so, but now we gon' have to fuck around and actually buy Mama a house out this way. All I hear nowadays is how she's clear across town from all her grandbabies," I mumbled.

"I guess you and your brothers better get a move on it then, because what Eva wants, Eva gets," Zo winked, stepping out onto the front terrace so I could lock the door behind us.

"Shit, who you tellin'? You gon' be aight though? I gotta run and handle something right quick before shit kicks off this afternoon. Zo's expression immediately shifted into a harsh grimace, and I knew what she was thinking. "Sis, come on, I ain't even on that. I meant what I said when I put that ring on Po's finger. I'm not about to fuck that up for nobody."

"Better not because Cloro's been itching to set some shit off since she touched down. I'll see you later, though."

I pulled my sister in law into a firm hug and brushed a quick peck on her cheek before we parted ways. I remember how when Zeus and Zo first started dating, her mere presence gave me a headache because she was so fuckin' alpha. She was cool as shit, but just not for my brother—at least that's what I thought. My opinion quickly changed the night she deaded that chick Snow, and it became clear she was just the type of chick Zeus could build with. Fuck being nice and polite, fuck decorum; Zo laid claim to what was hers and took no shorts.

Roughly an hour after leaving Zo, I was meeting up with a special connect to make a few moves before I headed to this extravagant ass baby shower that was planned to welcome the newest additions to the DiBiasi family. Today was the day we would all find out what Po was having, and I was looking forward to collecting my stacks and gloating in everyone's face. The whole family just knew that we were having girls, but fuck that. I knew we had two little DiBiasi men about to grace us with their presence, and I put money on it. I felt that shit in my bones!

Ж

The humidity outside was killer, but with so much family and love under one roof, it was a perfect day in my book. This was the first time we'd all been able to get together since shit kicked off with Santiago, and it felt so good to have our family back in Miami. Shit, even Cloro's mean ass was being all cordial and polite, and that was some shit for the history books.

"Thena, Perry! Time to take the stage, loves!" Cloro cheered as my nieces scampered up to the small stage that previously held the throne that was Po's seat of the day. Bones had strung up two piñatas from the elaborate pergola that Zo had installed just for today's festivities.

"Okay, doll faces. Here's your bat. Now, all you have to do is just keep swinging un—"

"Auntie Cloro, we got this." Athena winked, dismissing Cloro while sending the rest of us into a fit of laughter. Tori, Ares' girl, was laughing especially hard, and I smiled to myself at how happy they looked together.

My baby brother, the wild child, the one who kept Mama on the verge of a heart attack damn near all his life, had finally found *the one* that was official enough to tame his wild ass. There had to be a blizzard down in hell over this shit!

Athena and Perry let off a chorus of thumps as they swung their bats mercilessly at their assigned piñatas. Perry lost her footing at one point, but being the dutiful uncle he was, Ares sprang into action and caught her before she fell. Zo and Zeus sat off to the side, shaking their heads at the savagery of their daughters. These were truly little DiBiasis in the making, and I felt for whomever had the misfortune of ever crossing—

"The fuck?!"

My thoughts were interrupted when Athena dealt the final blow to rip her piñata to shreds, unleashing a swarm of pink confetti and individually wrapped pieces of candy.

"Ohhhhhhh shit! I told you, nigga! Pay the fuck up!" Ares sprang to his feet, talking much shit and boasting the five stacks he'd just won. Of course, all I wanted in the end was two healthy babies, but Ares was the worst nigga to lose a bet to, and I knew he'd be clowning and carrying on well after the babies were born behind this shit.

Not even a minute later, Perry ripped into her piñata, releasing a hail of blue confetti and candy into the air.

"Yooooooooo, I got a son! I'm gon' have a son!"

It was now my turn to spring into action as I pulled Po to her feet and twirled her around before pulling her in for a sloppy kiss.

"See, we both win." Po smiled, and she was right. She got her lil' girl, and I got my son. Life was good.

"Hold up, nigga—you still lost, so run me half of that," Ares frowned as I brushed his hand off.

"A little prince *and* a new little princess? The good Lord sure does answer prayers!" Mama cheered. She was seated right next to Po's parents, and Santos Orozco gave me a quick nod when our eyes met.

"Stand up right quick?" I urged Po, who had just reseated herself and was still gushing at the wave of excitement that had swallowed Zeus and Zo's backyard.

"T, my feet hurt," Po whined.

"That's what you get for tryin' to look cute today. Slip them heels off and come with me right quick."

Frustrated, she sighed before kicking her heels off and letting me lead her back up to the stage that was now littered with remnants of the blue and pink confetti Zeus and Zo's housekeeper had quickly swept away. A minute later, we were joined by the final guest whose arrival I had been eagerly awaiting.

"Father Rossi?" Zo was the first to speak up as Zeus gave me a baffled frown. All eyes were now on Po and me just as I'd hoped.

"Titan? What's going on?"

"Check it, we got the house, a king and queen on the way, the presence and love of both our families. There's just one thing missing, and we can fix that in 'bout..." I paused to look down at my watch. "Five minutes if you'll do me the honor of taking these vows with me today and officially becoming the next Mrs. DiBiasi."

I couldn't even finish my sentence good before Po was flooding the yard with tears of joy. Zo, Zeus, Cloro, Ares, Mama—shit, everybody's jaws were on the floor in shock at the pop-up wedding I had managed to pull together. The only people that knew the true purpose of us all coming together today were me, Father Rossi, and Santos; of course, I had to get his blessing to seal my future with Po. I didn't want him to feel like I was cheating his daughter out of a proper ceremony.

Aside from the piñata filling, the yard was decorated in white, gold, and lilac for the baby shower—the same color scheme Po always said she wanted on her wedding day. True, we could have held off and had a big, fancy wedding that would rival even the most posh celebrity wedding, but it wasn't all about that for me. My brothers and I had been to hell and back, took some unexpected losses, and felt our share of pain since we unknowingly stumbled into a war with Santiago.

The fact that we were able to come out of that shit alive with our families intact was reason enough to celebrate life to the fullest, and

I couldn't think of a better way for Po and me to make things official than in the presence of our families today and on the same day that we were celebrating our new son and daughter.

"You have declared your consent before the Church. May the Lord in his goodness strengthen your consent and fill you both with his blessings. What God has joined, men must not divide. Amen," Father Rossi spoke his final words over our union as our family confirmed their agreement and erupted into a round of applause and cheers.

"Love you, bighead," Po managed to speak through her sobbing.

"Love you back, Mrs. DiBiasi," I whispered before scooping her up and carrying her away from the stage.

"Shit, Titan! What are you doing?"

"Dippin' off with my wife to get some married pussy, girl. Fuck the honeymoon!"

CHAPTER 21

Ares

After all the hoopla surrounding Titan and Po's baby shower/ wedding, I knew that the pressure would be on for me to do the same. Now that Zeus and Titan were both married, my mother would be looking to marry me off to Tori soon, especially since we had a child on the way. Don't get me wrong, I had mad love for Tori, but a nigga wasn't ready to commit the rest of his life to her—not to anyone, for that matter. Though I've been keeping my dick out of other women, I wasn't ready to give up the possibility that I could. Just thinking about the shit gave me hives.

I sat in the chair next to the examination table, waiting on the doctor to come in to check Tori. Today, we were finally going to found out the sex of the little person growing inside of her belly. She wanted to do the whole gender reveal thing at the baby shower, but I wasn't about to wait to find out the gender of my seed. Fuck that, everybody else could wait, but I was too impatient for some shit like that. As impatient as I am, I was still scared to hear the results. Tori's mother swore that it would be a girl, but I was holding out a grain of hope that God would bless me with a little soldier.

"How are you feeling today, Ms. Brown?" Dr. Ankoma asked as she walked through the door.

I made sure to get Tori a female doctor because ain't nan nigga sticking his head or hands between her legs.

"I feel good," Tori smiled. "Just ready to see what our little munchkin will be."

"How about you, dad? You ready to see what you will be raising?"

"Of course."

"What are we hoping for?"

"He wants a son, but I'm hoping for a little princess."

"All we want is a healthy baby," I assured the doctor.

"Boy, stop," Tori smacked her lips.

Dr. Ankoma chuckled at us while gathering the equipment she needed to do the examination. I'm sure she heard the gender debate on a daily basis, so I wasn't going to start one up now when we were getting ready to get the answer.

I attentively watched the monitor while the doctor rolled her magic wand over Tori's belly. The only thing that I was looking for was a penis, and I still hadn't saw one yet. To be honest, I didn't know what the hell I was looking at, but I was sure I would know a lil' penis when I saw one.

"We have a strong heartbeat," Dr. Ankoma stated with her eyes still planted on the monitor. "The baby is growing beautifully, the perfect size for nineteen weeks. Now, if we can just get the little munchkin to open its legs, we can solve this mystery."

At that moment, I thought *damn, it's a girl.* If it was a boy, he would've been in there chillin' with his legs cocked wide open like me. That fact that the legs were closed tight made me think of a female and how they be sitting all prissy and shit.

"Okay, let's see what we have hiding in there," Dr. Ankoma spoke, making my stomach drop into my balls. "Looks like…we have a little… princess in there."

Tori's eyes shot up to me, and I couldn't help but smile. Although I wanted a lil' hitta on my team, I was happy about my princess as well. Immediately, my mind began to think about how many more guns I had to buy. With Tori's and my genes mixed together, we were sure 'nuff bringing a dime piece into this world. God forbid that she inherited these gray ass eyes I was blessed with. I leaned over Tori and planted a soft kiss on her lips. She had tears streaming down her face that I carefully wiped away with my thumb.

"Are you happy, baby?" I asked.

"Yes," she cried.

"We havin' a lil' mini you," I joked.

"As stubborn as she is, I think she will be a mini you."

"Even better," I smiled, then kissed her again.

"Okay, Ms. Brown, everything looks perfect so we're all done here. Don't forget to schedule your next appointment with the front desk, and congratulations."

"Thank you," we said in unison.

Dr. Ankoma stood up from her chair, then exited the room. I pulled Tori up by her arms to help her off the table. I look at Tori's sexy ass every day, but today she seemed to be even more beautiful to me. Could it have something to do with the fact that she was giving me a daughter? Or did shit finally just get real to me? I didn't know, but either way, it was time for me to start taking steps toward making us a family.

"You look so beautiful, baby," I kissed her.

"Even after finding out that I'm giving you a daughter?"

"Especially after finding out that you're giving me a daughter," I expressed while rubbing on her thighs.

"No, Ares."

"What?" I joked, sliding my hands further up her thighs.

"We're not fuckin' in this doctor's office."

"Why not? It's sterile in here."

"I'm not 'bout to play with you, Ares," she said, sliding off the table.

"Ain't gon' be no playing," I grabbed a handful of that ass. "I'm gon' be handlin' business."

"No Ares, not here."

"Booo," I sung. "You supposed to give it to me wherever."

"Normally, I would, but we got to come back to this office. I don't want to do the walk of shame and be embarrassed when I come back here."

"Scary cat," I kissed her cheek. "Let's get out of here."

My mother knew that we were finding out the sex of the baby today, so she offered to make lunch for us, also inviting Tori's mom, Ms. Tanya, over to join us. I already knew that they would try to get the answer out of us, but I was keeping my lips closed. If Tori wanted the family to wait, then that was what they had to do. My mother was slick with it, so I knew that she would stop at nothing to get me to reveal the sex. This lunch would probably turn into an interrogation, but I was up for the challenge; let's just see if Tori would be able to holdout.

When I pulled into my mother's driveway and parked, I noticed more than just Ms. Tanya's car out front. From the looks of it, both of my brothers were here, and I was sure that they brought their ladies along with them. We were definitely walking into a setup, so I had to warn Tori before we even stepped foot on the porch.

"Looks like the entire family is here."

"I thought it was just gonna be our mothers?" Tori questioned.

"Me too, but I should have known better. Are we tellin' them now, or are we gon' make 'em sweat a little longer?"

"Well, since the whole family is here, we may as well tell them."

"A'ight, but make 'em sweat a lil' bit."

"Okay," she giggled.

I jumped out of the car, then ran around to the other side to help her out. As we made our way toward the front door, it swung open and my mother was standing there with her hypnotizing grin plastered on her face. Though I was happy on the inside, I put my game face on to ensure that I wouldn't give her anything to run with.

The closer we got to the door, the further open it swung open, and Ms. Tanya was standing next to my mother. They were really going to gang up on our asses today.

"Tori," my mother said, greeting her with a hug. "You look *maravilloso*. Come on inside." While Tori leaned in to give her mother a hug, my mother hugged me as tightly as her arms would allow. "Ares, *mi hijo*, I'm so proud of you."

"All that butter you're pouring won't make me slip up and tell you anything, Ma."

"Oh, but it will," she chuckled, closing the front door behind us.

I could hear Athena and Perry arguing over Apollo before I even stepped around the corner. They'd always been on some Tom and Jerry type shit, but since Apollo came into the world, they both had to be the boss of him. When I stepped into the living room, Zeus was sitting in the middle of the sofa, watching Athena hold Apollo.

"Uncle Ares!" Perry called out, as she ran toward me.

"Ms. Perry," I sung, leaning down to pick her up. "What's going on?"

"When you gon' have yo' baby so I can play with it? I don't want to share Apollo no more."

"It's gonna be a girl anyway," Athena shot at Perry. "Daddy told Uncle T that you bang mad thots, now you got to taste some medicine. What do bang mad thots mean?"

I shot a look at Zeus—he was frowning and shaking his head *no* like he didn't say the shit. Athena was smart, but she wasn't gon' make up a story like that, so I knew his bitch ass said it.

"You sick, Uncle Ares?" Perry asked, looking at me all concerned.

"Nah," I laughed.

"Only in the head," Titan joked, walking into the living room. "'Sup, A?" I put Perry down so we could dap each other up.

"Ain't shit, brother."

"Zeus," I said, pointing at him. "Watch what you sayin' around my nieces, man."

"I ain't even—"

"Whateva, nigga."

"So, am I gon' be an uncle or an aunty, nigga," Titan interjected.

All three of us smirked at each other, then burst out laughing.

"Shut yo' stupid ass up," I laughed. "And we not tellin' yet."

"Well, you better get in there 'cause they're ganging up on Tori. You already know Mama's not gon' stop until she knows what it is."

"Ugh," I groaned, walking off. "It's too many damn women in this family!"

All the women were in the kitchen moving about, so I quietly walked in and stood inconspicuously against the wall. I didn't want to get jumped on, but I couldn't let them corner Tori by herself either.

"I don't understand why we got to wait," Ms. Tanya announced. "I mean, y'all already know. This is my first grandbaby, and I need to know so I can start buying stuff already. Is it a Chipmunk or a Chipette?"

"Mama," Tori whined.

"Just tell us already," Zo pushed.

"Y'all back up off my lady," I finally spoke up. "Come here baby, you don't have to take this abuse."

Tori rolled her neck at them before strutting my way. I stuck my tongue out at them, then grabbing her hand to escorted her up the stairs to the study. My dick had been jumping since we left the doctor's office, and I needed to burst a serious nut.

As soon as I closed the doors to the study, I picked Tori up and pinned her against it. She already knew what time is was because she grabbed my face to pull me in for a kiss. I unbuckled my pants, then turned to walked us toward the Cherrywood desk that sat in the far-left corner of the room. Once my shoes connected with the bottom of the desk, I sat Tori on top of it, then let my pants fall freely to the floor. She was rocking a knee length dress with no panties, so I pushed it up over her breasts, then eased my erection into her.

"Mm, baby," she smiled. "I've been waiting on this."

"You the one actin' all shy at the doctor's."

"Go deeper, baby," she grabbed my ass.

I tucked my arms under her thighs to pulled her closer to me. She laid back on the desk, causing the little belly that she had to poke out. I planted a kiss on her stomach, then threw her legs over my shoulders. Tori stretched her arms out to hold onto the desk while I went to work on that pussy.

"Gimme dat wet ass pussy!"

"Yes, daddy! Fuck me!"

"Fuck me back."

I climbed up on the desk and was met with a photo of my father. He was staring right at me—shit, it looked like he was shaking his head at me, too. I swear I could hear his voice telling me to get my nasty ass off his desk. That only fueled the fire inside of me, making me want to fuck for hours.

"Ares DiBiasi!" My mother's voice quaked, startling me. "*Chico repugnante!*"

"I'm not nasty," I called out as she slammed the door behind her.

Tori had her hands covering her face, like my mother didn't already know who she was. Shit, she's already pregnant, so she was fully aware that we were fucking. I knew that I would hear about this later, though. I think the perfect time to announce that we were having a baby girl would be after we emerged from the room. Something had to be done to divert the attention away from us.

"I was thinkin," I looked over at Tori as we washed up in the half bath. "We should go get the rest of your clothes."

"A-are you asking me to move in with you, Ares?"

"Sure—I mean, yes. I want you and my baby girl under the same roof as me. I need y'all to be first thing I see when I wake up, and the last thing before I close my eyes at night."

"It's not like I can fit them anymore anyway," she smirked, "So, I can leave them there."

"Cool." Tori and I were practically living together anyway, but it was best that I made it official for her. "And, you can redecorate it if you want to."

She smiled, "I love you, Ares."

"I love you, too, Tori." She gasped. "Don't get all dramatic on me; yeah, I said that shit."

"I'm not trying to cry," she fanned her face. "I just can't make it stop."

"You good. Let's get out of here."

By the time we made it back to the kitchen, everyone was seated at the table, waiting on us. Without saying a word, I pulled Tori's chair out for her to sit, then took my seat next to her. All eyes were on us, but we both kept our lips tight.

"Will y'all just tell us already!" Zeus slammed his hand on the table.

"It's a girl," Po announced.

"How you know?" Titan questioned.

"'Cause, we all know Ares. If it was a boy, he would've came in here with his nuts out, acting a damn fool. He's been on chill mode all day."

"Is it?" Ms. Tanya clasped her hands together.

"Yes, Ma." Tori cheered. "We got our girl!"

"Told ya," Titan stood up and slapped Zeus five. "Pay up."

"Nah, don't give that nigga nothing." I pointed at Titan. "That nigga still owe me."

"Congratulations, boy," Titan reach over to slap me five.

Joy, congrats, cheers, and tears filled the room straight DiBiasi style. Zeus started passing around cigars while Titan poured up glasses of wine—for those who could drink. Our mother sat at the head of the table, smiling as she looked around at each one of us. Her family tree was growing rapidly, and that was what she'd always wanted. She had always wished for a boatload of grandchildren to keep her company in her old age. Being that she only had boys, she was more than excited about all of her granddaughters. I had to admit that I was excited too. I couldn't wait to see our kids growing up together and groom them to take over the empire one day.

EPILOGUE

Nine Months Later

"*D*addy, watch me!" Perry squealed with delight as she did a cannon ball into our swimming pool.

"Good job, baby!" I cheered her on as I held a babbling Apollo over my shoulder. He was almost ten months old, and my lil' nigga was fat as shit.

"Look at yo' ass being a cheerleader and shit," Ares joked when I sat down on the lounge chair next to him.

"Shit, nigga, just wait. Yo' ass gon' be cheering on your little one, too. Don't let this shit fool you; I'll still murk a nigga," I retorted.

"That's why his ass been walking around like the Grim Reaper; he misses the streets," Titan said, sitting down with his twins, Achilles and Acacia.

Achilles looked just like Titan's ass. Titan always started grinning like a muthafucka anytime someone said it. Achilles was his pride and joy. Po was not playing when she said that she wanted a mini-her, because Acacia looked and acted just like Po's ass. You couldn't tell her little ass that she didn't run shit. She had been trying to hold her head up since she made her appearance in the world. Acacia had Titan wrapped around her finger, though. If she cried, that nigga would break the sound barrier to get to her.

"Since we dealt with Santiago, ain't nobody fucking with us like that," I said, bouncing Apollo on my knee. He was trying to get his ass down so he could go mess in some shit. I swear, ever since that little nigga started crawling, he has gotten into everything.

"Yeah, I feel you on that shit. Except for smacking around a couple of crack heads, my Glock ain't seen no action," Ares agreed.

"And you won't be seeing no action," Tori butted in. "The only action you gon' be seeing is changing diapers."

Tori placed their baby girl, Eres, in his arms. I smiled at the fact that Ares' wild ass was even gentle enough to hold an infant, but lil' mama had him wrapped around her finger. She was only a few weeks younger than Titan's twins, so she definitely would have some playmates. My mother was having a field day with all her new grandbabies. She rotated between all our homes every three days to lend a hand. She was in hog heaven.

"That's all I'm saying," Po agreed, taking Acacia from Titan.

"You ladies got the game fucked up," Zo finally said. She took Apollo from me and kissed his fat cheeks before taking a seat at the edge of the pool. "You want them to let off that steam? Shit, that's when I get the best d-i-c-k," she joked with a wicked smile.

"Mama, what's dick?" Athena asked, causing Zo to turn red and frown at her.

"It's something you won't be getting until your ass is forty," I scolded her with a frown. "Get out of grown folks' business, Athena. Go swim."

Athena shrugged her shoulders and hopped in the pool. I watched her as she waded over to Perry and a couple other neighborhood kids.

"It seems to me that you need to stop getting d-i-c-k," Po whispered with a smirk. "Don't you have something to tell your husband?"

"What are you talking about?" I asked with a raised eyebrow.

"Guess who's pregnant," Tori instigated.

"Oh, shit. Don't tell us yo' ass pregnant again, Zo," Ares said with a roll of the eyes.

"I bet she is. Zeus tryna raise a small village," Titan joked.

"So what if I am pregnant? We got the money," Zo said, flipping her long hair over her shoulder. "Shit, I could adopt a few too."

"Zo, baby, is you is or is you ain't about to have my baby?" I asked, even though I already knew the answer.

"Yeah, Zeus." She rolled her eyes. "I was just getting my body back, but I guess I'mma have another one of your big-headed babies."

I almost dislocated my jaw because my smile was so big. Zo could have a million of my babies, and I would be the happiest man on earth. Shit was finally winding down for the DiBiasis, and we could not have been happier. My player ass brothers were settling down and bringing seeds into the world. They were finally growing up, and I knew they would be alright. Shit, I taught them a lot of what they knew.

When I finally decided to retire, we had our little hittas that would be groomed and ready to fuck some shit up. Life was fucking spectacular.

THE END

Looking for a publishing home?

Royalty Publishing House, Where the Royals reside, is accepting submissions for writers in the urban fiction genre. If you're interested, submit the first 3-4 chapters with your synopsis to submissions@royaltypublishinghouse.com.

Check out our website for more information: www.royaltypublishinghouse.com.

Text ROYALTY to 42828 to join our mailing list!

To submit a manuscript for our review, email us at submissions@royaltypublishinghouse.com

Text RPHCHRISTIAN to 22828 for our CHRISTIAN ROMANCE novels!

Text RPHROMANCE to 22828 for our INTERRACIAL ROMANCE novels!

Do You Like CELEBRITY GOSSIP?

Check Out QUEEN DYNASTY!
Visit Our Site: www.thequeendynasty.com

Get LiT!

Download the LiT eReader app today and enjoy exclusive content, free books, and more

CPSIA information can be obtained
at www.ICGtesting.com
Printed in the USA
LVOW10s2122100417
530296LV00015B/651/P